HEAT

MIKE
LUPICA

PHILOMEL BOOKS

ACKNOWLEDGMENTS

I would like to first thank Lourdes LeBatard,
who so generously helped me with the beautiful words of Cuba.
Additional thanks go out to all the Little League baseball coaches
from whom I have learned along the way, from the great
Cliff McFeely to Kevin Rafalski. And to all the other coaches who
understand what Michael Arroyo does in the pages of this book:
The game belongs to the kids playing it.
Finally, Michael Green: Who always had a clear,
fine vision of what should be happening on both sides of
those blue barriers outside Yankee Stadium.

PHILOMEL BOOKS A division of Penguin Young Readers Group. Published by The Penguin Group. Penguin Group (USA) Inc., 375 Hudson Street, New York, NY 10014, U.S.A. Penguin Group (Canada), 90 Eglinton Avenue East, Suite 700, Toronto, Ontario, Canada M4P 2Y3 (a division of Pearson Penguin Canada Inc.) Penguin Books Ltd, 80 Strand, London WC2R 0RL, England. Penguin Ireland, 25 St. Stephen's Green, Dublin 2, Ireland (a division of Penguin Books Ltd.) Penguin Group (Australia), 250 Camberwell Road, Camberwell, Victoria 3124, Australia (a division of Pearson Australia Group Pty Ltd). Penguin Books India Pvt Ltd, 11 Community Centre, Panchsheel Park, New Delhi-110 017, India. Penguin Group (NZ), Cnr Airborne and Rosedale Roads, Albany, Auckland 1310, New Zealand (a division of Pearson New Zealand Ltd). Penguin Books (South Africa) (Pty) Ltd, 24 Sturdee Avenue, Rosebank, Johannesburg 2196, South Africa. Penguin Books Ltd, Registered Offices: 80 Strand, London WC2R 0RL, England.

 Published simultaneously in Canada. Printed in the United States of America. Design by Gina DiMassi. Text set in Charter. Library of Congress Cataloging-in-Publication Data Lupica, Mike. Heat / Mike Lupica. p. cm. Summary: Pitching prodigy Michael Arroyo is on the run from social services after being banned from playing Little League baseball because rival coaches doubt he is only twelve years old and he has no parents to offer them proof. [1. Brothers—Fiction. 2. Orphans—Fiction. 3. Illegal aliens—Fiction. 4. Cubans—Fiction. 5. Little League baseball—Fiction. 6. Baseball—Fiction. 7. Social service—Fiction.] I. Title. PZ7.L97914Hea 2006
[Fic]—dc22 2005013521 ISBN 0-399-24301-1

7 9 10 8

This book is for Taylor Lupica.
She has always believed in me,
and that I should be writing books
children want to read.

It is also for our own amazing children:
Christopher, Alex, Zach, and Hannah.
They have not just made me a better person.
They have made me a better writer.

1

Mrs. Cora walked slowly up River Avenue in the summer heat, secure within the boundaries of her world. The great ballpark, Yankee Stadium, was on her right. The blue subway tracks were above her, the tracks colliding up there with the roar of the train as it pulled into the station across the street from the Stadium, at 161st Street and River.

The two constants in my life, Mrs. Cora thought: baseball and the thump thump thump of another train, like my own personal rap music.

She had her green purse over her arm, the one that was supposed to look more expensive than it really was, the one the boys upstairs had bought for her birthday. Inside the purse, in the bank envelope, was the one hundred dollars—Quik Cash, they called it—she had just gotten from a Bank of New York ATM. Her food money. But she was suddenly too tired to go back to the Imperial Market. Mrs. C, as the kids in her building called her, was preparing for what could feel like the toughest part of her whole day, the walk back up the hill to 825 Gerard from the Stadium.

Now she moved past all the stores selling Yankees merchandise—Stan's Sports World, Stan the Man's Kids and Ladies, Stan the Man's Baseball World—wondering as she did sometimes if there was some famous Yankee who had been named Stan.

He hit her from behind.

She was in front of Stan's Bar and Restaurant, suddenly falling to her right, onto the sidewalk in front of the window as she felt the green purse being pulled from her arm, as if whoever it was didn't care if he took Mrs. Cora's arm with it.

Mrs. Cora hit the ground hard, rolled on her side, feeling dizzy, but turning herself to watch this . . . what? This boy not much bigger than some of the boys at 825 Gerard? Watched him sprint down River Avenue as if faster than the train that was right over her head this very minute, pulling into the elevated Yankee Stadium stop.

Mrs. Cora tried to make herself heard over the roar of the 4 train.

"Stop," Mrs. Cora said.

Then, as loud as she could manage: "Stop, thief!"

There were people reaching down to help her now, neighborhood people she was sure, voices asking if she was all right, if anything was broken.

All Mrs. Cora could do was point toward 161st Street.

"My food money," she said, her voice cracking.

Then a man's voice above her was yelling, "Police!"

Mrs. Cora looked past the crowd starting to form around her, saw a policeman come down the steps from the subway platform, saw him look right at her, and then the flash of the boy making a left around what she knew was the far outfield part of the Stadium.

The policeman started running, too.

The thief's name was Ramon.

He was not the smartest sixteen-year-old in the South Bronx. Not even close to being the smartest, mostly because he had always treated school like some sort of hobby. He was not the laziest, either, this he knew, because there were boys his age who spent much more time on the street corner and sitting on the stoop than he did. But he was lazy enough, and hated the idea of work even more than he hated the idea of school, which is why he preferred to occasionally get his spending money stealing purses and handbags like the Hulk-green one he had in his hand right now.

As far as Ramon could tell at this point in his life, the only real job skill he had was this:

He was fast.

He had been a young soccer star of the neighborhood in his early teens, just across the way on the fields of Joseph Yancy park, those fields a blur to him right now as he ran on the sidewalk at the back end of Yankee Stadium, on his way to the cobblestones of Ruppert Place, which ran down toward home plate.

"Stop! Police!" Ramon heard from behind him.

He looked around, saw the fat cop starting to chase him, wobbling like a car with a flat tire.

Fat chance, Ramon thought.

Ramon's plan was simple: He would cut across Ruppert Place and run down the hill to Macombs Dam Park, across the basketball courts there, then across the green expanse of outfield that the two ballfields shared there. Then he would hop the fence at the far end of Macombs Dam Park and run underneath the overpass for the exit from the Deegan Expressway, one of the Stadium exits.

And then Ramon would be gone, working his way back toward the neighborhoods to the north, with all their signs pointing toward the George Washington Bridge, finding a quiet place to count his profits and decide which girl he would spend them on tonight.

"Stop . . . I mean it!" the fat cop yelled.

Ramon looked over his shoulder, saw that the cop was already falling behind, trying to chase and yell and speak into the walkie-talkie he had in his right hand all at once. It made Ramon want to laugh his head off, even as he ran. No cop had ever caught him and no cop ever would, unless they had begun recruiting Olympic sprinters for the New York Police Department. He imagined himself as a sprinter now, felt his arms and legs pumping, thought of the old Cuban sprinter his father used to tell him about.

Juan something?

No, no.

Juantarena.

Alberto Juantarena.

His father said it was like watching a god run. And his father, the old fool, wasn't even Cuban, he was Dominican. The only Dominican who wanted to talk about track stars instead of baseball.

Whatever.

Ramon ran now, across the green grass of Macombs Dam Park, where boys played catch in the July morning, ran toward the fence underneath the overpass.

It wasn't even noon yet, Ramon thought, and I've already earned a whole day's pay.

He felt the sharp pain in the back of his head in that moment, like a rock hitting him back there.

Then Ramon went down like somebody had tackled him from behind.

What the . . . ?

Ramon, who wasn't much of a thinker, tried to think what had just happened to him, but his head hurt too much.

Then he went out.

When the thief opened his eyes, his hands were already cuffed in front of him.

The fat policeman stood with a skinny boy, a tall, skinny boy with long arms and long fingers attached to them, wearing a Yankees T-shirt, a baseball glove under his arm.

"What's your name, kid?"

The one on the ground said, "Ramon," thinking the policeman was talking to him.

The cop looked down, as if he'd forgotten Ramon was there. "Wasn't talking to you."

"Michael," the skinny boy said. "Michael Arroyo."

"And you're telling me you got him with this from home plate?"

The cop held up a baseball that looked older than the old Stadium that rose behind them to the sky.

"Got lucky, I guess," Michael said.

The cop smiled, rolling the ball around in his hand.

"You lefty or righty?"

Now Michael smiled and held up his left hand, like he was a boy with the right answer in class.

"Home plate to dead center?" the cop said.

Michael nodded, like now the cop had come up with the right answer.

"You got some arm, kid," the cop said.

"That's what they tell me," Michael said.

2

PAPI WAS THE FIRST TO TELL MICHAEL ARROYO HE HAD THE ARM.

Michael thought it was just something a father would say to a son. But he knew there was a look Papi would get when he said it, as though he were seeing things Michael couldn't, back when it was just the two of them playing catch on that poor excuse of a field behind their apartment building in Pinar del Rio, outside of Havana.

Back home—what Michael still thought of as home, he couldn't help himself—everybody knew his father as Victor Arroyo. But he was Papi to Michael and his brother, Carlos. Always had been, always would be.

"You cannot teach somebody to have an arm like yours," Papi would say, walking out from behind the plate and sticking the ball back inside Michael's glove. Like they were having a conference on the mound during a game. "It's something you are born with, a gift from the gods, like a singer's voice. Or a boxer's left hand. Or an artist's brush."

This was when Michael was seven years old, maybe eight, long before they got on the boat that night last year, the one that took them across the water to a place on the Florida map called Big Pine Key. . . .

"Someday," Papi would say, "you will make it to the World Series, like the brothers Hernandez did. But before that, my son, what comes first?"

Michael always knew what the answer was supposed to be.

"First, the Little League World Series," he would say to his father.

"On ESPN," Papi would say, grinning at him. "The worldwide leader in sports."

Papi always made it sound as if that was supposed to be Michael's first great dream in baseball, to make it to the Little League World Series in Williamsport, Pennsylvania—Papi always showing him Pennsylvania on the ancient spinning globe they kept in the living room—for the world's championship of eleven- and twelve-year-old baseball boys.

Michael knew better, even then.

Michael knew that it was more his father's dream than his own. Papi had grown up in a time when a star Cuban baseball player, which Michael knew Papi sure had been as a young man, could never think about escaping to America, the way others would later, the most prominent lately being the Yankee pitcher Ricardo Gonzalez. El Grande, as he was known. So Papi, a shortstop on the national team in his day, never made it out, never made the great stage of the major leagues.

He became a coach of Little League boys instead, in charge of grooming them even then to become stars later for Castro's national team.

And from the time he saw that Michael had the arm, he had talked about the two of them traveling to Williamsport together and having their games shown around the world.

Even now, Michael couldn't tell where Papi's dream ended and his own began.

The dream had moved, of course, from Pinar del Rio to the Bronx, New York. Papi was no longer his coach and Michael was no longer a little boy. He had grown into the tallest player on his team during the regular season, and now the tallest on his All-Star team.

It was the All-Star team from the Bronx that Michael's left

arm was supposed to take all the way to Williamsport in a few weeks.

As long as he didn't get found out first.

His brother Carlos had promised they could have a catch behind the building when he finished his day shift at the Imperial, the food market across 161st Street next to McDonald's, almost directly underneath the subway platform.

This was before Carlos went off to his night job, the one he said had him busing tables at Hector's Bronx Café, a few stops up on the 4 train. Carlos said he had lied about his age to get the job at Hector's, telling them he was eighteen already, and no one had bothered to ask him for a birth certificate. The main reason for that, Carlos had told Michael, was that he was being paid off the books. Making it sound like a secret mission almost.

"What does that mean, off the books?" Michael had asked.

Carlos said, "It means, little brother, that this is the perfect job for me, at least for the time being. In the eyes of Official Persons, I don't even exist."

Carlos was always talking about Official Persons as if they were the bad guys in some television show.

Now, cooking their Saturday morning breakfast of pancakes and *chorizo,* their Cuban sausage, Carlos smiled at his brother and said, "My little brother, Miguel, the hero of the South Bronx."

"Guataca," Michael said. Flatterer.

"Just eat your breakfast," Carlos said. "You're turning into a freaking scarecrow, Miguel. Even thinner than a *birijita.*"

It was a Cuban expression for a thin person.

In the small, rundown apartment, their conversation was always a combination of Spanish and English. Their old life and their new one. It was only here, when it was just the two of them, that

Carlos would ever call his little brother by his birth name—Miguel. To everyone else, it was always Michael.

Michael still thought of Havana as home, because he was born there. And he had been Miguel Arroyo there.

Here, he was Michael.

"You're not exactly a heavyweight boxer yourself," Michael said.

"I have an excuse," Carlos said, "running from one job to another."

"And then running from table to table, right?" Michael said.

Carlos smiled at him. "Right," he said. "Like I am passing plates in a relay race instead of the baton."

"Maybe I could get a job," Michael said.

Carlos laughed. "And maybe you're too busy fighting crime, somehow turning baseballs into guided missiles."

"I told you," Michael said, "it was a lucky throw. I saw him running, I heard the policeman . . ."

"Then you just managed to hit him in the back of his hard head from . . . how many feet away?"

Michael grinned. "The trick is leading him just right." He jumped up from his chair, his mouth full, made a throwing motion. "Like a quarterback leading his favorite wide receiver." Then he added, "If I'd known it was that purse you got for Mrs. C on her birthday, I would have run after him and hit him with a bat."

"Mrs. C is telling the whole building you were meant to be on the field, like you were an angel," Carlos said.

"The only Angels are in the American League West," Michael said, "with halos on their caps." He poured more Aunt Jemima syrup on his stack with a flourish, finishing as though dotting an *i*. "If there are real angels in the world," Michael said to his brother, "how come they're never around when we need them?"

"Don't talk like that." Putting some snap into his voice, like he was snapping a towel at Michael.

Michael looked over and saw him at the counter, opening an envelope, making a face, tossing it in a drawer.

"Why not? It's true," Michael said.

"Papi said if we had all the answers we wouldn't have anything to ask God later."

"I want to ask Him things now."

"Eat your pancakes," Carlos said, then changed the subject, asking if there was All-Star practice today. Michael said no, but a bunch of the guys were going to meet at Macombs Dam Park before the Yankee game.

"It must be a national TV game," Carlos said, "if it's at four o'clock. Who's pitching, by the way?"

"He is."

"El Grande? I thought he just pitched Wednesday in Cleveland."

"Tuesday," Michael said. "Today is his scheduled day."

"That means another sellout."

"The Yankees sell out every game now."

"It just seems like they squeeze more people in when El Grande pitches," Carlos said. "What's his record now since his family came? Five-and-oh?"

"Six-and-oh, with an earned run average of one point four five."

"Before the season is over, we'll get two tickets and watch him pitch in person," Carlos said. "I promise."

"You know we can't afford them."

"Don't tell me what we can and can't afford," Carlos said, slamming his palm down on the counter, not just snapping now.

Yelling.

It happened more and more these days, Carlos exploding this

way when he was on his way to one of his jobs, like a burst of thunder out of nowhere, one you didn't even know was coming.

"Sorry," Michael said, lowering his eyes.

Carlos came right over, put a hand on Michael's shoulder. "No, Miguel, I'm the one who's sorry. I'm a little tired today, is all."

"We're cool," Michael said.

"That's right," Carlos said. "Who's cooler than the Arroyo boys?"

He said he was going to get dressed for work, but had to pull out the stupid ironing board and iron his stupid Imperial Market shirt first. The one he said looked as if it should belong to a bowling team. When he was gone from the kitchen, Michael went over and quietly opened the drawer where Carlos had thrown the envelope.

It was their Con Ed bill. The same bill Carlos had been slamming in a drawer for the past three months.

We *do* need an angel, Michael thought.

Michael read the *Daily News* when his brother was gone, going over the box scores of last night's games as if studying for a math test. Then he listened to sports radio, to all the excited voices talking about how this would be a play-off atmosphere this afternoon, because the Yankees and Red Sox were tied for first place in the American League East.

At least this was a Yankee game Michael would be able to watch on his own television. When it was a cable game, on the Yankees' own network, he would occasionally ask Mrs. Cora if he could watch at her apartment, if there was nothing special on she wanted to watch. She would always say yes. Mostly, Michael knew, because she liked the company, even if she didn't really like baseball. Michael knew Mrs. Cora had a daughter who had run off young, but she didn't talk about her too often, so Michael didn't ask.

Sometimes, with Carlos's permission, he would go and watch the night games at his friend Manny's apartment, a few blocks up near the Bronx County Courthouse, as long as Manny's mother would walk him home afterward.

Carlos promised they would get cable the way he promised they would get to see El Grande pitch in person.

There were all kinds of dreams in this apartment, Michael thought.

Sometimes he didn't care whether the game was on television or not, even if his man was on the mound. Michael would take his transistor radio and go outside on the fire escape, the one that was on the side of the building facing 158th Street, and sit facing the Stadium and listen to the crowd as much as he did to the real Yankee announcers, hearing the cheers float out of the top of the place and race straight up the hill to where he sat.

From there, not even one hundred yards away, he could see the outside white wall of Yankee Stadium and the design at the top that reminded Michael of some kind of white picket fence. The opening there, he knew, was way up above right field, pennants for the Mariners and Angels and Oakland Athletics blowing in the baseball breezes.

Just down the street, and a world away.

Michael Arroyo would sit here and when the announcers would talk about El Grande Gonzalez going into his windup, the windup that Michael could imitate perfectly even though he was left-handed and El Grande was right-handed, he would be able to imagine everything.

Michael's teammates called him Little Grande sometimes, even though he was bigger than most of them.

The ones who spoke Spanish called him *El Grandecito*.

He didn't even try to understand why throwing a baseball came this easily to him, why he could throw it as hard as he did and put it where he wanted most of the time, whether he was pitching to a net or to the other twelve-year-old stars of the South Bronx Clippers, named in honor of the Yankees' top farm team, the Columbus Clippers.

Michael Arroyo just knew that when he was rolling a ball around in his left hand, before he would put it in his glove and then duck his head behind that glove the way El Grande did, everything felt right in his world.

He wasn't mad at anyone or worried about what might happen to him and his brother.

Or have the list of questions he wanted to ask God.

Papi would never stand for that, anyway. Papi always said, "If you only ask God 'why?' when bad things happen, how come you don't ask Him the same question about all the good?"

As always, Michael imagined Papi here with him now, using that soft old catcher's mitt of his, the Johnny Bench model, whipping the ball back to Michael, telling him, "Now you're pitching, my son," that big smile on his face under what Michael always thought of as his Zorro mustache.

And every few pitches he would take his hand out of the Johnny Bench mitt and give it a shake and say, "Did I just touch a hot stove?"

They would both laugh then.

Michael couldn't remember all of Papi's pet sayings, no matter how hard he tried. Mostly he remembered the way it felt when they were just having a game of catch, everything feeling as good and right to him as a baseball held lightly in his hand.

The way it did now, just sitting alone in the apartment, the way he was alone a lot these days, rolling the ball around in his hands, feeling the seams, trying different grips. Sometimes when he held a ball like this on the mound, before he would go into his motion, Michael could trick himself into believing everything was right in his world. Sometimes.

The phone rang.

Michael didn't even move to answer it, knowing the house rule—Rule Number One—about never answering the phone when Carlos wasn't here, just letting the ancient answering machine, the one with Papi's voice, pick up.

Michael wanted to change the outgoing message, but Carlos said, no, it sounded better that way.

The voice on the other end belonged to Mr. Minaya, his coach with the Clippers.

"Mr. Arroyo," Mr. Minaya began, because he called all the parents Mr. or Mrs. "You don't have to get right back to me, but once we get to the play-offs, we're going to need parents to drive to the game and since, well, you are a professional driver, we were wondering if you might be able to help out. Please let me know."

Michael waited for the click that meant he had disconnected. But he wasn't finished.

"Unless of course Mr. Arroyo isn't back yet and I'm talking to Carlos and Michael . . . well, forget it. Just tell your dad to give me a call if he ever does get back."

Then came the click.

If he ever does get back.

Not when.

Does he suspect something?

Michael grabbed his glove off the kitchen table where he'd left it, stuffed the ball in the pocket, locked the apartment door behind him, headed for the field at Macombs Dam Park.

The field had always felt like his own safe place. But now Michael wondered if even baseball was safe.

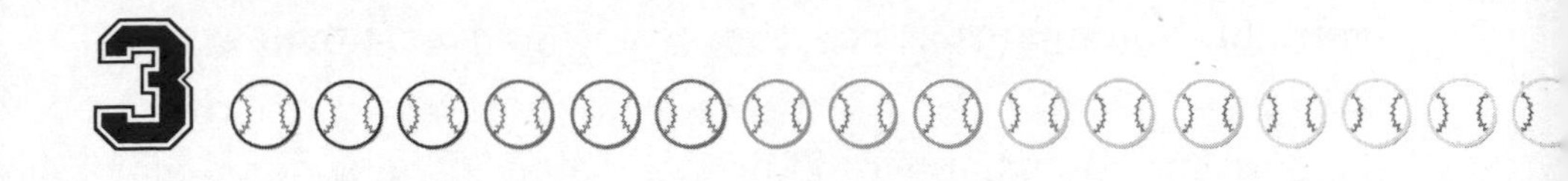

THERE WERE TWO BALLFIELDS AT MACOMBS DAM PARK, A REAL GREEN-GRASS park in the Bronx.

The regulation diamond, one with big-league dimensions used by Babe Ruth teams and American Legion teams and even some high schools, was tucked in the corner of the park where 161st Street intersected with Ruppert Place. The Little League field was the one closer to the Major Deegan Expressway.

During the regular Little League season, Michael's first in America, his team was sponsored by the big New York sporting goods store, Modell's—they called themselves the Modell Monuments, after the monuments inside the Stadium—and played its home games here. Now, in the summer, the Clippers also played their home games at Macombs, when they weren't playing other Bronx All-Star teams, up in Riverdale and at Castle Hill Field and at Crotona Park, maybe a mile away by car from Gerard Avenue. Sometimes they would play games as far away as White Plains and New Rochelle, because there were even All-Star teams from south Westchester County in their district, District 22.

On summer days, the kind that seemed to have no clock on them except for the setting sun, the kind you never wanted to end, Michael and his friends usually had the Macombs Dam Park field to themselves, if they could get up enough guys for a pickup game. Even if they couldn't come up with two full teams, they would invent games, depending on how many players they had.

On days like this, baseball would make Michael as happy as it ever did. No umpires. No coaches. No rules except the ones you made up.

Just play, on what felt to Michael like his own personal playground.

Other times they would join the older kids on the regulation field, though Michael would never pitch in those games, from the mound sixty feet from home plate, because Carlos had forbidden that. So had Mr. Minaya.

"You can move back from home plate when you move up to the thirteen-year-olds next season," Mr. Minaya had said.

The only other player from the Monuments who had made the Clippers, the South Bronx All-Star team that would eventually try to qualify as the representative of the eastern states to go to Williamsport for the World Series, was his catcher, Manny. Manny was waiting now, along with two other guys from the Clippers, Kelvin Carter and Anthony Fierro, on the back field when Michael showed up.

It was still only two o'clock, two hours from when El Grande would pitch against the Red Sox, but already you could see more traffic getting off the Deegan above them, see the whole area around the Stadium coming to life, as it always did on game day.

Manny smiled when he saw Michael. Nothing unusual about that. Manny Cabrera always seemed to be smiling, except when he would strike out with the bases loaded, or when he would fail to throw out a runner trying to steal second base. He was almost a head shorter than Michael, twenty pounds heavier at least, and was the best catcher in all of District 22.

Some of the players on the other team would occasionally call him No Neck Cabrera, mostly because he didn't have one. Usually they did this when they thought he couldn't hear them. But even when he did, he still had that smile on his face, as if he and the world were in on the same joke.

"Here comes the superhero now," Manny said as Michael walked across the infield.

"Whoo whoo whoo," Kelvin said, pumping his fist.

"Which X-Man is he? I forget," Anthony Fierro said.

"Wish he was that fine X-Girl, Halle Berry," Kel said.

Then Kel whoo whoo whoo'd again, but it seemed to be more for Halle Berry this time than Michael.

"Do not start," Michael said.

"Oooh, listen to the starting pitcher, telling us not to start," Manny said, like a comedian playing to a crowd of three. "Maybe he's afraid we'll reveal his secret identity."

Kelvin Carter was the Clippers' shortstop. His father worked on the grounds crew at Yankee Stadium, which meant he was one of the guys who did the little dance routine to the song "YMCA" when it was time to rake the infield dirt in the fifth inning.

Kelvin said, "Dude catches criminals by day, does his bad Little League thing by night."

"Better not let Coach find out you threw it from home plate to dead center," Manny said.

"Who said I did?" Michael said.

"I think I heard it from Katie Couric," Manny said.

"No," Kel said, "it had to be Oprah!"

"I definitely heard about it from Dan Patrick on SportsCenter," Anthony said.

"Shut up," Michael said, unable to keep a smile down. "All of you."

"I can't believe it wasn't on the front page of the *Daily News,*" Anthony said.

Michael knew there was no sense fighting them when they got going like this. The best thing to do was let them have their fun until they ran out of what they thought were hysterically funny lines.

"Okay, we'll stop," Manny said eventually. "But before we do, I have to ask you one question."

He got up from the bench, put his catcher's mitt on, which meant he was ready to start getting Michael warmed up.

"Knock yourself out," Michael said.

Manny looked at Kelvin and Anthony, both of whom were already giggling.

He said, "When you are fighting crime—what color cape do you wear?"

Howls.

Kelvin said, "Or do you wear those tights like Spider-Man and Daredevil and them?"

"Whoa, not Daredevil," Manny said, "the girl in that movie, the one from *Alias,* she took out more bad guys than Ben Affleck did."

Michael was throwing a ball high into the air, straight up, and catching it, sometimes behind his back, doing his best to ignore them.

"You know," he said finally, as if talking to the sky, "maybe the real Daredevil will be the guy who has to lead off against me today."

Everybody made a low whooooooo sound.

"In that case," Manny said, "it's a good thing Kel begged to hit first today."

"Did not," Kelvin said.

"Did, too."

"Did not infinity," Kel said, as if slam-dunking the word *infinity*. "That's the only time I'd ever ask to hit against Arroyo, by the way. On the twelfth of infinity."

"I promise I won't throw hard," Michael said, heading for the mound as Manny got into his squat behind home plate.

Kelvin was still shaking his head as he watched the guys going out into the field, deserting him. "Your half speed is faster than most guys' full speed, Arroyo. So don't be givin' me none of your 'I won't throw hard.' "

He reluctantly went over to the screen behind home plate where they'd all stacked their bats.

"Just don't be trying for the magic number today," he said.

"Eight-zero," Manny said.

The past couple of years, there had been more and more games from the Little League World Series on television, starting with the sectional qualifiers. Manny's family had cable, so he would invite Michael over to their apartment to watch the games on ESPN and ESPN2, and they would talk about this year, the year when they were sure they would make it far enough in the tournament to get on TV themselves. And in all the games they had watched—and Manny watched a lot more than Michael did—there had never been a time when one of the pitchers' fastballs had been measured at eighty miles an hour.

They had seen Danny Almonte, the star pitcher from another Bronx team, the kid who got even more famous when they found out he was fourteen instead of twelve the year he was pitching all his no-hitters, get to seventy-five miles an hour. Manny said he remembered someone he described as a big old boy from Kentucky putting up what he called a double-seven.

But no one had ever hit eighty.

Eighty was the magic number for Little League pitchers the way 100 was for radar guns in the big leagues. Except, Manny said, hitting 80 at their age was really the same as someone older hitting

110. That was his theory. Manny had theories about almost everything under the sun, Michael knew.

Here was another:

That Michael hit eighty all the time, even if they didn't have television cameras or radar guns covering the Modell Monuments, or the Clippers. Manny said that he didn't need no stinking gun for his Pudge Rodriguez mitt to know how fast Michael was throwing.

Kel had his bright red batting gloves on, but was still complaining about having to be the first to hit, making it sound as if they were sending him to detention. Or the principal's office. When he was finally done, he heard Manny call out to Michael, "Let me give you a sign." Manny put down one finger, which meant fastball.

Kel whipped his head around. "I saw that," he said. "You told him to throw his number one, didn't you?"

"Maybe I did, maybe I didn't," Manny said.

During the game sometimes, he would put down two fingers, or three, or even four, but that was just for fun, like a game he and Michael played with each other. Or if there was a runner on second base who had watched too much big-league baseball on television and thought it mattered if you stole a sign and knew what pitch was coming. But Michael and Manny knew that Michael's dad had told him he wasn't allowed to throw any kind of curve until he was in high school, it was bad for his arm. Not just his arm, but any arm, Papi had always said, attached to a Little Leaguer's body. So Michael didn't even fool around with curves when he was fooling around with his buddies like this.

Papi had drilled the dangers of breaking balls into him, from as far back as Michael could remember, the way he had drilled English into him.

Or the dangers of drugs.

So sometimes Michael would take something off his number

one, just as a way of setting a hitter up or getting him off balance, provided it was one of the handful of hitters he'd run into who could actually get around on his fastball.

Michael threw fastballs for six innings a week, which is all the innings Little League rules allowed him to pitch in one week. Mr. Minaya could break up those six innings any way he wanted. Michael could pitch six in one game, or three in two games. Or four one day and two a couple of days later.

Just no more than six a week in the regular season.

But this wasn't official pitching now, not against Manny and Kel and Anthony. This was just pure fun, from his first pitch, which he lobbed up there to Kel. Who looked shocked as he put his bat on the ball and hit one in the air to where Anthony was standing in short center field. Michael wanted Kel to hit a few balls to Anthony, just so Anthony would stop complaining about not having any balls to shag.

"I should have brought my homework," Anthony had said when he first got to the outfield, refusing to move more than ten yards back from second base.

"You don't do homework," Manny reminded him.

"Well, if I did," Anthony said, "this would be a perfect time to catch up on it."

After a few lob balls Kel said, "Okay, I don't want anymore of your pity, go ahead and gun it."

Michael made a show of rubbing up the old ball they were using. "First you don't want to hit because you say I throw too hard. Now you say I'm throwing too easy. You're giving me . . . Manny, what's he giving me here? You're the one with the words."

"A mixed message."

"Exactly," Michael said. "You're giving me a mixed message."

Kel, smiling out at him, made a show like he was about to give

Michael an upraised middle finger. "Like to give you something more than that," Kel said.

"Hey," Michael said, "there could be kids watching."

"I thought we were kids," Manny said.

"Nah," Kel said, "we're much cooler than that."

"We are soooooo cool," Manny said.

"Cooler than LL Cool J," Kel said.

Anthony, who had the deepest voice of all of them, had come into the infield. Now he made his voice even deeper, trying to make himself sound like a TV announcer. "Hey," he said, "all you South Bronx Clippers, where are you going as soon as you kick a little more butt?"

"Disney World?" Kel said.

Anthony made a sound like a game-show buzzer that meant, wrong answer.

"Where are we going?" he asked again.

In one voice, Anthony's included, they yelled, "Williamsport!"

Anthony ran back out to center. Manny got back into his squat. Then Michael threw a real number one to Kel that he missed by a mile, as if he were swinging at the sound of the ball going past him, not at anything he saw.

That wasn't the best part of the pitch.

The best part of the pitch was that Michael's best buddy Manny, who thought he was used to Michael's heat, who bragged on being the only guy in District 22 who could even think about handling Michael's heat, got knocked back so hard from the force of the pitch that he ended up sitting down.

Michael started in from the mound. "Are you okay?" he said.

"Fine," Manny said.

He just sat there as if nothing had happened, perfectly relaxed, staring at the ball in his glove. "Absolutely fine," he said.

Then he popped to his feet. Manny was agile for someone with a body shaped like a fire hydrant. Only Michael, of all his friends and teammates, knew about the dance classes he took, the ones he even admitted to Michael he liked, because they were a way for him to show off how light he was on his feet, not just some lump behind the plate. The guy who stayed in one place for so much of a baseball game loved to move, Michael knew.

He brought the ball out to the mound himself, handed it to Michael, said, "Eighty."

Michael looked around. "Did I miss the guy with the Jugs gun?" It was one of the first radar guns he'd ever heard them talking about on radio.

"I told you," Manny said. "I don't need no stinkin' gun."

He put his Pudge mitt between him and Michael. "I got this," he said. "And this never lies."

He yelled at Anthony Fierro to come in and hit if he wanted, then walked back to the plate.

"Eighty," Michael heard him say.

Some other ballplayers from the neighborhood, Babe Ruth League kids, showed up just as Michael and Manny and Anthony and Kel were about to pack it in and go to McDonald's. Then some older kids who'd been shooting baskets on one of the courts over near the Stadium asked if they could play. That made it thirteen players in all, enough to have a game. Three infielders, two outfielders, a pitcher. Manny had offered to be full-time catcher, saying he didn't need to hit, he'd already conquered hitting.

Michael played center field, saying he might throw a couple of pitches at the end, just for fun. But he loved playing center field, loved getting a chance to run across the outfield and pretend it was inside the Stadium.

Michael loved to move, basically.

So they played their pickup game, trash-talking each other, laughing, barely keeping track of the score, everybody trying their hardest to smoke balls past the two outfielders or, in the case of the bigger kids from the basketball court, trying to jack balls over their heads. When they were waiting to hit they could look past the batter's box, toward Yankee Stadium, and see the baseball afternoon coming to life now, gathering force like one of the late-afternoon storms you got in the summer. Occasionally they would hear the cheers from the fans lined up behind blue police barriers on both sides of the players' entrance to the Stadium as the players walked out of their parking lot on the Deegan side of Ruppert.

Michael was able to picture it in his head because of all the times he had come and stood behind those blue barriers himself, hoping to get a look at El Grande, even four hours before game time, knowing El Grande liked to get to the park early when it was his turn to pitch.

So Michael was fairly certain that El Grande Gonzalez was already inside the Yankee clubhouse by the time the Clippers and the rest of the kids on the far field at Macombs were playing their pickup game, one they had agreed at the start would be five innings. It turned out the four basketball guys had bleacher tickets to today's game, which they proudly showed off to Michael and Manny, bragging, pulling the tickets out of the pockets of their baggy gym shorts, shorts that went way past their knees, as if they were pulling out pieces of gold. But in the meantime, they had their own game to play.

It was in the top of the fourth inning that Michael noticed the beautiful girl watching them through the fence at the basketball court.

Michael was twelve, and a boy, and a ballplayer, and usually showed no interest in girls because he knew his friends would act as if he had broken some kind of law. But even Michael Arroyo could see this was an uncommonly beautiful girl, with long dark hair and dark skin and big, dark eyes that somehow, even from a distance, looked sad to him.

The girl had a baseball glove under her arm.

Maybe she's sad, he thought to himself, because we haven't asked her to play.

The girl was still watching through the fence when it was Michael's turn to pitch in the top of the fifth.

For some reason, he looked over at her after his first pitch to the tallest of the basketball players, the one whose name was Eric Scopetta, whose nickname was E-Scope.

E-Scope was a banger. He'd already proved that when Kel had pitched to him, hitting a bomb to the place in dead center where there was a hole in the fence, the one the purse thief had been running toward before Michael took him down with a bomb of his own.

Now Michael went into his full windup, his El Grande windup, leg high, his ball and his head tucked briefly behind his glove, before he threw a fastball past E-Scope that made the older boy not only miss, but put very colorful swear words together, in a way Michael had never heard before, not even living in the Bronx, where you could walk past an open window in the summer and feel as if you'd discovered the capital of swearing.

Michael ignored him, looked back toward the fence, wanting to see if the pretty girl was still watching, if she'd seen him pour his fastball in that way.

She was watching. And no longer looked sad. She had her arms folded in front of her, the glove pressed against her chest, and Michael was sure she was laughing at him.

As if she had been waiting for him to look back over so he could see her laughing at him.

It was almost as if she knew—in that way that girls always seemed to know things that boys didn't—that he wouldn't be able to help himself, that he needed to see what her reaction would be.

But what the heck was so funny?

Michael struck out E-Scope on three pitches, struck out the next two guys not even throwing his hardest, jogged in to the bench, and put his glove down. He had made the last out the inning before, so it would be a while before he hit, if he hit at all, since this was his team's last ups.

He told Manny he'd be right back, and started walking toward the basketball courts. Not walking toward the girl at first. Walking with his hands in his pockets, head down, as if he were on his way to the small brick administration building for Macombs Dam Park, up at the corner of 161st and Ruppert.

But when he got about twenty yards away, he turned and started walking toward her, smiling at her now, calling out to her.

"Hey," he said. "What was so funny before?"

And that's when she ran.

She was wearing a white T-shirt and blue jeans and had legs almost as long as Michael's. Tall, pretty girl.

With those eyes.

She ran, fast for a girl, for *anybody,* up the hill toward Yankee Stadium, her glove under her arm, until she disappeared into the crowd of people coming around the corner from the subway station, all those who had their own tickets like gold in their pockets to watch El Grande high-kick his fastball into gear against the Red Sox.

Gone.

4

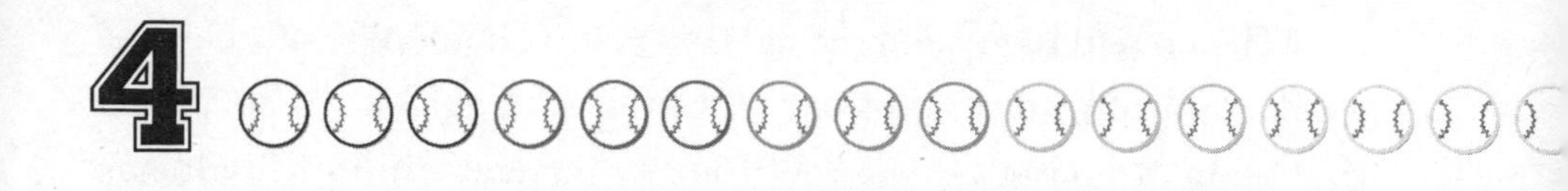

THE FOLLOWING DAY, AFTER MICHAEL CAME HOME FROM CHURCH WITH MRS. Cora, what had become a Sunday ritual with them, he read all about El Grande's shutout of the Red Sox in the *Daily News* and the *Post.* It was a way for him to experience that game all over again, even if he had seen every single pitch of the complete game in which El Grande gave the Red Sox just four singles, struck out ten, and walked just one batter.

The stories in the paper reminded everybody that El Grande, who had struggled in April, had not lost a game since his family had finally made it out of Cuba a month before, made it across the waters of the Florida Straits the way Papi and Carlos and Michael had two years before.

El Grande's wife and two children had made it despite the fact that the Coast Guard had picked them up twenty miles south of Key West in the middle of the night and chased them until dawn with three fast boats and a helicopter. All those Official Persons on the water in the night, Carlos said, smiling and shaking his head as he did, and they had still been unable to catch the spider boat with El Grande's people on it.

"That wasn't a high-speed chase on the high seas," Carlos had said when they watched the eleven o'clock news that night. "That was a police escort."

Michael had asked what he meant. It was the same with Carlos as it was with Manny Cabrera:

Sometimes it was as if they were speaking to Michael in code.

"They must have been tipped that they had the wife and kids of a star Yankee pitcher on board," Carlos had said. "I'm surprised they didn't let that boat go all the way to the Harlem River and drop everybody off a few blocks from the ballpark." Carlos was smiling that night, in a good mood, as he put his arm around his younger brother. "We should have told them the night we came that we had the famous pitcher Miguel Arroyo on board."

Carlos finally woke up around noon, took a shower, got dressed, and announced he was taking Michael out to lunch at McDonald's. While they were there, both of them having two double cheeseburgers with fries and chocolate shakes, Carlos asked when Michael's game was.

"Two o'clock," Michael said. "Against the best team from Westchester."

"I'm there," Carlos said.

Michael shook his head. "It's your one day off," he said. "You don't have to come and watch me pitch a dopey Little League game."

"Yes," Carlos said. "I do." He had already inhaled his first double cheese and was getting ready to start on his second. "How many innings for you today?" he asked Michael.

"The last four. We got rained out against Eastchester on Thursday, remember? And I only pitched two innings last Tuesday when we lost to Fordham Road."

"They must be good if they can beat you guys," Carlos said.

"They are," Michael said.

"Well, I will see you over there, little brother," Carlos said. "I haven't gotten to see you pitch four straight innings in a month."

When they were finished eating, Carlos cleaned up everything—plastic trays and garbage and cups. Maybe he thinks he's still on the job at Hector's, Michael thought. But lately Carlos tried to be very organized about everything. Always wanting to show Michael he was in charge. On top of everything. Even when it came to busing a table at what all of Michael's friends called Mickey D's.

Michael knew it was just his brother's way of acting older than he really was.

Like he was Papi Jr.

When he came back to the table, he told Michael to sit for one more minute, he had something he wanted to talk about.

"Sounds serious," Michael said. "Did I leave a towel on the floor of my room?"

Carlos said, "You did, slob face. But that's not what I want to talk to you about."

Michael waited.

Carlos leaned forward, made his fingers into a steeple, put them under his chin. Another grown-up pose of his. "I just want to remind you that as you and the other guys on the All-Stars continue to win games, there's going to be more attention drawn to you. Which means," Carlos said, "you're going to have to be more careful about what you say, who you say it to."

"I don't need reminding," Michael said.

"I know you don't," Carlos said. "You're smart, even if you are a slob. But you just have to keep it at the front of your brain that the bigger the games, the bigger the spotlight."

Carlos made the spotlight sound like one more thing for them to be afraid of.

His brother walked him back to the apartment, then told him he had some errands to run. Michael said it was Sunday, he should be resting instead of running errands, especially if he was coming to the game in an hour.

Carlos said for him to go rest himself for an hour or so, he'd see him later, in the top of the third.

• • •

Michael faced thirteen batters from Westchester South.

He struck out ten.

The Westchester team managed only one hit off him, on a little blooper that died in front of Kel at short, and then bounced away from him for an infield hit. The only other ball in play was a little roller their cleanup hitter, a blond kid almost as tall as Michael and looking a lot heavier, hit about halfway to the mound in the top of the third. Earlier in the game, the same kid had hit a three-run homer off Anthony Fierro, the ball just clearing the left-field fence. They were the last runs Westchester would get in the 4–3 loss.

The blond-haired kid didn't like looking foolish, and even tried to convince the home plate ump that the dribbler he'd hit back to Michael had ricocheted off his foot first.

"It was a foul ball," the kid kept saying in a loud voice until Manny took off his mask and said, "In your dreams maybe."

The blond kid said, "What's that supposed to mean?"

Manny just smiled, trying to let the kid know this wasn't something worth fighting about. "Hey, dude, you did good just getting your bat on the ball, don't be looking for a do-over."

The best comeback the blond kid, clearly the star of his team, could manage was: "I wasn't talking to you."

But Manny was talking to him, and once Manny got started it was hard—more like impossible—for him to stop. He walked out, dug the tip of his spike into the grass about where Michael had picked up the blond kid's roller. "The way my man is pitching today, this is the same as going deep on his butt."

"Maybe he is a man," the blond kid had said. "He throws like one."

It occurred to Michael that they were discussing him as if he weren't there.

The Westchester kid said, "How old is he, anyway?"

It was, Michael knew, like giving Manny a pitch he could drive.

Manny said, "Twelve years, two months, five days, and however many hours it was until you were a lucky boy to even touch the best fastball you're ever going to see."

The blond kid, dug in good now, said, "He doesn't throw it like any twelve-year-old I've ever seen."

Manny gave the big jerk a smile that seemed to stretch from the Deegan to the subway tracks over River Avenue. "No, he does not." Then he turned his head, spit, went back behind the plate and got into his crouch.

In the top of the sixth, trying to make sure the Clippers held on to their one-run lead, Michael had struck out the side on ten pitches. Of course the last hitter up turned out to be the blond kid, whose name, they had heard by then, was Justin.

"You can't get any more white-bread than bein' a Justin," Kel had said on the bench when they all heard the Westchester coach call the blond boy by name.

Manny would say later that the one called ball Michael had thrown old Justin, the one with two strikes on him, should have been a strike, too, but the ump had taken pity on the poor guy, not wanting to end the game on a punch-out.

The ump had come out to clean off home plate after he called the pitch a ball. While he did, according to Manny, he looked up at Justin and in a real quiet voice said, "You better be swinging on the next one, son."

Justin did swing. From his heels.

But Michael blew the ball right by him.

Ball game.

At that point, Justin threw his bat against the back screen. The ump hadn't wasted any time, calling out the Westchester coach and telling him that his star was suspended from the next game. The coach said that only happened if you got ejected, and that the ump couldn't eject somebody from a game that was already over.

"Watch me," the ump answered.

That was when Justin started yelling, as his coach tried to pull him away. The ump immediately pulled out his cell phone. The coach asked who he was calling. "The league commissioner," the ump said. "I want him to hear every word of this."

That was when Justin finally shut up.

At that point Michael got into line with the rest of the Clippers, shaking hands with the Westchester players, all except Justin, who somehow managed to veer off and head back to his bench just before he got next to Michael, staring hard at him from a distance, still acting more ticked off at Michael than he was at the umpire who'd just clipped him for a game.

"He can't be that mad just because I got him out," Michael said to Manny.

"He must think it's impossible for anybody his own age to make him look like that much of a girl."

"Hey," Michael said, "not so loud. We have a girl, remember? And she's *good*."

They did. Maria Cuellar, whose parents were Puerto Rican, was the second fastest player on their team, after Kel. She played second base, could play third or short if she had to, and could hit.

"I don't think of Maria as a girl," Manny said. "I think of her as one of us."

"Really?" Michael said. "I watch you sometimes watching her, and you don't seem to look at her the way you do our other infielders."

Manny turned to Michael, no expression on his face whatsoever, his voice completely calm, and said: "Shut up about Maria."

"I'm good with that."

Manny said, "Just so we're clear."

Mr. Minaya gathered them out in right field for a few minutes the way he always did after games, went over what he liked about what they'd done today, what he didn't like, told them what he told them after every game: That the object was to have fun, but to learn something every single time they went out there.

"You never know what thing you learn might make the difference between making it to Williamsport and watching the games from your sofa," he said.

It had already reached the point in the season, Michael and his teammates knew, where Mr. Minaya wasn't really interested in whether or not they were having fun, that was just his cover story. He wanted to make it to the World Series as much as any kid on his team. Maybe more.

Sometimes when Mr. Minaya got going about the World Series he sounded a lot like Papi, which meant he made Williamsport, Pennsylvania, that ballpark you'd see on television with happy parents in the stands and no highways in the distance, sound like baseball heaven. . . .

"Did you hear me, Michael? Or were you in Williamsport already?"

"I was, actually," Michael said. "Sorry, Coach."

"I was asking if anybody needed a ride over to Crotona Park on Tuesday night," Mr. Minaya said.

Michael looked down at his old baseball shoes, that hole in the toe of his left one, as he said, "I could use a ride."

There was a pause before Mr. Minaya said, "Can't your father bring you?"

Michael, trying not to look nervous, said, "No."

"He's still not back from Florida?"

Michael shook his head.

"I wondered why he hadn't called me back."

"It's still just Carlos and me," Michael said. "But Mrs. Cora looks out for us."

Mr. Minaya said he would swing by and pick Michael up at four-thirty. Michael said he'd be out front. Mr. Minaya said, "I hope your uncle gets better soon, it would be a shame if your father misses our first play-off games after missing the whole regular season."

Michael just nodded and told Mr. Minaya he would see him on Tuesday, told Manny he could call him later, picked up his glove and bat, and started walking fast in the direction of the Stadium. Then he was running, jogging at first, but then sprinting, just wanting to get home to the apartment, afraid to look back, afraid they might still be watching him.

He didn't want Mr. Minaya or his teammates to see him crying.

About the father that had been dead since May.

5

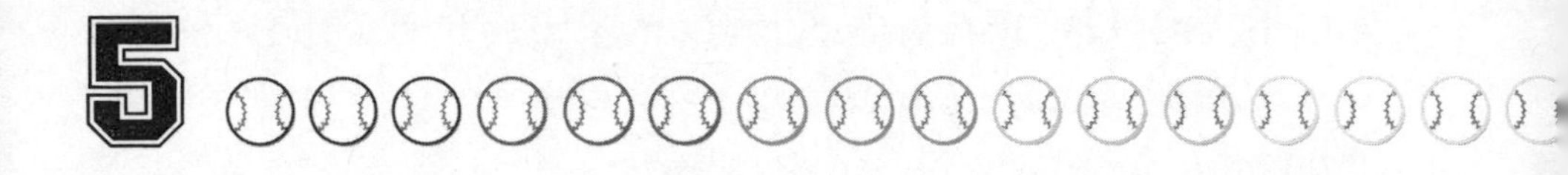

MICHAEL REMEMBERED HOW HIS FATHER USED TO LAUGH WHEN HE'D HEAR one of the sports announcers say something about how heart could only carry an athlete, or a team, so far.

"Little do they know," he'd say.

Then he'd give two little taps to his chest, the way the big-league ballplayers did sometimes just after they'd hit a home run.

Their grandfather, Papi's father, had died young of something to do with his heart, and so had their great-grandfather. Papi had never made a secret of that. And once, back in Havana when Michael was five or six, Papi had been in the hospital for a few days with what their mother described as a "mild attack to the heart."

Papi laughed off that one, too.

"Mild," he said, "usually means it attacked somebody else's heart."

Then he would tell them not to worry, he would not only die an old man, he would die in America.

It turned out he was half right.

Some of it Papi told Mrs. Cora himself, when he made it back to her apartment that day.

Some of it Carlos found out later on his own, because he said he had to know.

All of it became their secret.

Their father had been driving his gypsy cab on Kingsbridge Road, the middle of May, right before Memorial Day weekend. His fare was a woman. Papi let her off in front of her apartment building, and she paid him. It was a beautiful day, and so he had the windows down, and just as he was pulling away, he heard shouting from behind him.

A man had been waiting for the woman.

An ex-boyfriend, Carlos would find out later.

Papi stopped his Crown Vic, the one with a hundred thousand miles on it, watching the argument now as well as listening to it.

He saw the man raise a hand to the woman, knock her to the ground.

"The rule is that once they are out of the car, they are no longer your responsibility," he said later to Mrs. Cora. "But that was not my rule."

Papi got out of the car, yelled at the man to stop. The man turned and yelled at him to mind his own business. The woman on the ground was crying. When Papi came up on them, the man took one swing before Papi put him down. A neighbor would tell Carlos this part. The man got up, tried to charge Papi like a bull.

But Papi put him down again.

That's when he felt something grab in his chest.

"He tells me this as he begins to fade," Mrs. C later told Michael and Carlos, "like an old photograph."

The woman later told Carlos when he went to visit her that she had thought something was wrong with the kind cabdriver then, but he had told her he was just too old to be engaging in schoolyard fights. At this point, the woman's ex-boyfriend had had enough and ran off. Papi told the woman to call the police and got into his car and drove away. Papi, even in America, had always warned his sons, you never want to spend too much time talking to the police.

He managed to drive home, getting back to their building just as Mrs. Cora was coming back from noon mass. Papi told her he felt as if a bomb had gone off inside his chest. She took him inside to her apartment.

"I am dying," he said.

The way he said it, a look he had, told Mrs. C he was telling her the truth.

"Let me call a doctor," she said.

"No," he said. "A priest. One who will keep my secret."

"What secret?" Mrs. Cora said.

"The secret," he said, "that I am gone."

It was already too late for the priest. Papi held on to Mrs. Cora's hand, telling her, "Keep my boys together." His last words.

Then he died.

Father Montoya came and gave him the last rites. Mrs. Cora told him that he was to tell no one, not even at the church, about Papi's death. He asked why. She said because those were the father's wishes, that if something he had called the Family Court found out the boys had no parents and no relatives, they would come for them.

Mrs. Cora said to the boys later, "The priest asked who would take care of you two. I told him you would take care of yourselves."

The super had a cousin who ran a funeral home over near Kennedy Airport in Queens. He handled the details of the burial, at a small cemetery near the Aqueduct Racetrack.

Father Montoya drove Carlos, Michael, and Mrs. C.

The boys used the emergency money they knew their father had kept in a box in the cupboard to buy a cheap casket. They made sure that the man from the funeral home put Papi's old catcher's mitt inside with him.

And the new ball he and Michael had played catch with the day before he died.

They came home and Carlos went looking for work. Mrs. Cora said she would adopt them as her foster children if she could. But her late husband had never bothered to get his papers. And besides, she barely had enough money of her own to live on. Papi had no brothers or sisters. Their mother, the one who had died so young of cancer Michael could not even remember her, had sisters still living in Cuba, but neither Carlos nor Michael had spoken to them in years, or had any idea how to get in touch with them. From the time their mother had died, it had just been the three of them, father and two sons.

The father who had always told them he was going to die old and die free, until his own great heart could only carry him so far.

"Maybe some family could adopt the two of us," Michael said one night, when Carlos was at the kitchen table, figuring out again how much money they would need to get by once the last of Papi's emergency money ran out.

"One teenaged boy and another about to be a teenager?" Carlos said. "Maybe there is that kind of family on a TV show, in the TV world. But not in the real world." He shook his head. "No, we just have to find a way to get by until I turn eighteen."

"That's not until next spring," Michael said.

"Little brother," Carlos said, "believe me, if I could change my birth certificate, I would."

"Will they really separate us if they find out?"

"I can only tell you what I read, mostly on the Internet," Carlos said. "There is something where they say they would try to keep siblings together. But they can't guarantee it. If someone finds out about Papi, then we go into Family Court. And after that, little brother? Then it's up to them. The Official Persons. If they can't place us in a foster home, then we could go into a group home. Maybe even back to Cuba."

"I want to stay here," Michael said. "This is our home."

Carlos got up from the table, came over, hugged him hard.

"And it's going to stay our home, Miguel. We are going to stay a family, and we are going to live in this apartment until you graduate from high school and the Yankees come and offer you a big bonus contract and then . . ."

"What?"

"Then we live happily ever after in America, the way Papi promised."

"You think we can keep everybody from finding out?"

"Do we have a choice?"

Michael said, "I'm afraid."

It was something he would never admit to Manny, or the other Clippers, or even Mrs. C.

"Let me worry," Carlos said. "You just pitch."

So they came up with the story, any time anybody would ask, that Papi had gone to visit a sick brother in Key West, Florida, and that Mrs. C was looking out for them. Whenever someone new would ask, Carlos would just tell them that Papi had only been gone a couple of days.

This had gone on for three months. Carlos worked, and worried. Michael pitched.

A family of three had become, in Michael Arroyo's young mind, an army of two.

6

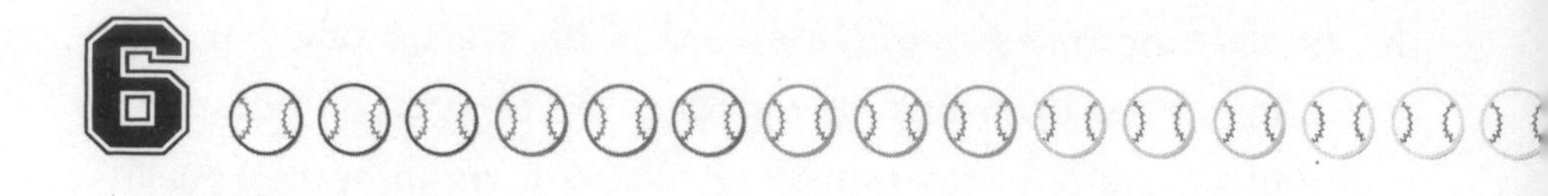

THE GIRL SHOWED UP AGAIN.

It was two days after the Crotona game, which the Clippers had won, 3–2. Michael had pitched the first three innings, struck out eight of the nine batters he faced before handing the ball, and the game, over to Anthony Fierro and watching Anthony pitch his best three innings of his All-Star season from there.

There was no game or practice scheduled for the next day, but Manny told Michael he'd meet him at Macombs after his doctor's appointment for his stupid allergies, somewhere around three o'clock. Michael knew that could mean anywhere between three and four. He operated on Manny Standard Time, and there was no getting around it if you were Manny Cabrera's friend. He was loyal, funny, smarter than he let on, loved baseball as much as Michael. There were so many good points with Manny that Michael couldn't keep track of them all.

But none of Manny's good points, not a single one, involved him showing up on time for anything except a real game.

So instead of going straight down to the field, Michael decided to stop at the Stadium first. That night the Yankees were going to play the last game of an eleven-game home stand, El Grande on the mound. Michael had found a brand-new ball in the apartment, stuck it in the pocket of his glove, stuck a Magic Marker in his pocket, and walked around the Stadium to where the blue barriers had been set up near the Yankees' souvenir store, the one with so many of the players' jerseys in the front window.

El Grande's number 33 was front and center. Michael had heard the radio announcers saying the other day that it was currently outselling all the other Yankees jerseys combined.

As usual, most of the people waiting for the players to arrive were adults, carrying their own balls and programs and photographs and notebooks. Carlos had once said these were the people who only wanted autographs so they could turn around and sell them.

"But if you were lucky enough to get your favorite player to sign something," Michael had said, "why would you sell it?"

"Because baseball is a business to these people," Carlos answered. "Even a signature from one of their heroes."

"It's different with me," Michael said.

"And always will be," Carlos said.

Now, behind the blue barriers, Michael slithered to the front of the crowd as the people around him cheered and called out to Joe Johnson, the Yankee first baseman, and the rookie catcher, Tony DiVeronica, short and squat, built like an older version of Manny. Out of the parking lot after them came the new Japanese right fielder, Sazaki.

No El Grande.

Michael watched as a few more players arrived, a couple of the Yankee broadcasters. Finally he asked a boy about his age if El Grande had arrived yet.

"You missed him by like ten minutes," the boy said. "But it wouldn't have done you any good, the guy walked right past us like we weren't even here."

Michael said, "He's pitching tonight, he probably doesn't stop to sign on days when he's pitching."

"Dream on," the other boy said. "I've never seen the guy even look over here."

Dream on, Michael thought to himself, and made his way across

Ruppert Place and across the basketball courts to wait for Manny. Who actually showed up at three-thirty, almost on time if you were using Manny Standard Time.

"Before you say anything, my arm hurts from my shot," Manny said.

"Did the shot make you walk slower getting here?"

"It's not your fastball I'm going to remember someday," Manny said. "It's your compassion."

"I'm sorry about the shots," Michael said. "Really. Though if they'd give it to you in your butt, you probably wouldn't have felt anything."

"Ha ha," Manny said. "Ha ha ha."

He went and got behind the plate without being asked. Michael knew by now that it was the same with Manny the catcher as Manny his friend: He would do anything for Michael. On or off the field. It was never something the two of them discussed, or that required a thank-you from Michael. But if he announced right now that he wanted to throw pitches to Manny Cabrera for an hour straight, Manny would just nod. And in an hour, would still be snapping back throws to Michael out of his crouch as if Michael had just thrown his first pitch of the day. He'd still be yelling, "Now you're humming, bud."

He wouldn't even think about stopping until Michael did.

This was one of the moments when he wanted to thank Manny, or at least try, even if he knew he wouldn't get anywhere, because he never had in the past.

"You know," Michael said, "I don't think I could even think about pulling this thing off without you. . . ."

They both knew how much trouble Manny would be in if his mom ever found out the secret Manny was keeping, knew from Carlos that any adult who found out about two children living without an adult was supposed to report them, by law, to something called the Administration for Children's Services. Manny didn't want to hear about it.

"Shut up and pitch," he said.

Michael did, getting himself loose, keeping track of the number of warm-up pitches he'd thrown before starting to cut loose, throwing as hard as he could before long, somehow becoming more accurate as he did, hitting Manny's mitt wherever he had it set up. Inside corner, outside corner, high in the strike zone, low, it didn't matter. Michael hit the glove almost every time.

Manny finally stood up, soft-tossed the ball back to Michael.

"You might not need a break, Star," he said, "Star" being his personal nickname for Michael. "But I do. Let's get a drink."

Michael said he was cool with that and began walking in from the mound. Manny waited for him at home plate. When Michael got there, Manny was looking past him, toward the outfield. Grinning. "Check it out," he said.

"Check what out?"

"We have an audience," Manny said.

Michael turned around.

There she was, out behind the center-field fence.

Staring right at him.

He still had the ball in his left hand. And without thinking about it he planted himself, wound up, and chucked the ball all the way out there, an even longer throw than he made to get the purse stealer. Put it on one bounce over the fence to where she was standing.

He stood there now with his hands on his hips. Hoping she could see him smiling at her.

The girl, in her long-legged blue jeans, wearing a pink T-shirt today that had something written on the front, walked calmly around the fence, like she had all the time in the world. Or: Like she was waiting to decide just what she wanted to do.

When she got to the ball, she looked at him. Then put her hands on her hips, like she was mimicking him.

Then the pretty mystery girl with the long legs picked the ball up and threw it back to Michael.

On the fly.

Michael turned around and looked at Manny. Who was staring at the girl in the distance the way you stare at fireworks the first time you see them in the sky.

"I saw," Manny said.

Michael stepped back behind the plate now—to show her his arm was better?—and threw the ball back, really gunning it, putting everything he had into it, like he was trying to throw it into the river. Wanting to make sure he got this one over the fence without any bounces.

The ball tracked on the mystery girl all the way, like it was a fly ball in a video baseball game that you were carefully guiding into an outfielder's glove.

When it got to her, she reached up, casual, like a big-league outfielder making a routine out, and caught the ball in her glove, one he hadn't even noticed she had on.

From behind Michael, Manny said, "Can of corn."

Michael barely heard him, he was staring at the girl still, wondering where the two of them were going with the strangest game of catch he'd ever played.

"You ever seen an arm like that on somebody our age?" Michael said finally.

"Yeah," Manny said. "Yours."

"Who is she?" Michael said.

"Just a girl," Manny said, "with Superboy's arm."

"A girl I've seen twice now," Michael said. "I didn't mention it, just 'cause I didn't think it was important, but she was watching us on Saturday when we were messing around in that pickup game."

"With that guy E-Scope?"

"Yeah."

"You talk to her?"

"I was going to, because I swear, I thought she was laughing when I was pitching to him that day. Like she found it funny."

"Well, dude, maybe she just noticed how funny you looked, even from a distance," Manny said.

"Very funny," Michael said. "And don't call me dude."

They looked over. She was watching them, keeping her distance still, throwing the ball up in the air.

Catching it with her glove behind her back.

Michael held up his glove. Telling her, Throw it back.

She did.

On the fly, again.

She was right-handed. She had, Michael could see, a beautiful motion, graceful, as if it wasn't taking any effort at all to throw the ball as far as she was throwing it. Inside his own head, not wanting to give Manny any kind of opening, Michael thought:

She definitely does not throw like a girl.

"We gotta meet her," he said.

"Okay," Manny said, "but let me do the talking."

Michael said, "What's that supposed to mean?"

"It means that you do not possess the ability to talk to girls in any sort of coherent manner."

"Coherent manner?" Michael said. "Did you get that out of one of your books?"

Manny Cabrera, Michael knew, didn't just love baseball and

dancing and watching movies. And maybe Maria Cuellar. He loved to read, too, even if that was another secret he kept from their teammates. He loved to read books that weren't even assigned on their Summer Reading list. So he was always dropping what sounded like grown-up expressions on Michael.

Manny shook his head now. "Actually," he said, "Jim Kaat used that one with Michael Kay on the Yankee game the other day, saying that when there's a runner on second who could be stealing signs, Joe Johnson doesn't always put down his signs in what would be considered a coherent manner."

"Whatever," Michael said. "And I can too talk to girls. I talk to Maria more than you do."

"I'm talking about talking to girls you don't know," Manny said. "Which is when you turn into one of those guys in the scary movies who can't even get their screams out."

"Do not."

"Do," Manny said. "Infinity."

Michael looked back over at the mystery girl. She was still there.

"Let's go, before she disappears again," Michael said.

The two of them started walking toward her.

She didn't run this time.

7

HER T-SHIRT READ:

Girls Rule.
Boys Drool.

She said her name was Ellie.

"Ellie Garcia," she said, and then gave them a look Michael couldn't read, as if she knew something they didn't. Or was just trying to act mysterious, which is something girls did all the time.

Manny said they couldn't help it, it was in their DNA.

After Manny handled the introductions for them, Michael said, "You didn't try to escape today."

"I didn't run away the other day. I was just late to be somewhere."

Up close, she was the most beautiful girl Michael had ever seen. This, he knew, was an observation coming from a boy who had no real interest in girls, other than his usual observation about them, which was how different they were from guys. "That will change, sooner than you think," Carlos always said when they'd have a conversation about girls. "I have no time for them," Michael would say back and Carlos would laugh and say, "Oh, you'll make time."

Michael wasn't so sure about that. All he knew with this girl right in front of him, not a hundred yards away now, was this:

Ellie Garcia was different from all the other girls.

"How old are you?" he said in a voice as loud as a door slamming.

Ellie jumped as if Michael had yelled directly into her ear.

Manny put a hand on Michael's shoulder. "Someday," he said, "my friend's dream is to host his own interview show on television. I would say like *Total Request Live,* except he doesn't watch MTV. No baseball highlights."

"Very funny," Michael said.

He felt himself coloring the way he knew he did when he was embarrassed. Manny liked to say it turned his coloring from baseball glove to New York Mets orange.

Ellie smiled. "I turned twelve last month."

Her accent, Michael noticed, was slightly heavier than his own. But pretty somehow. The way she was.

"Where are you from?" Michael said.

"The interview continues," Manny said.

"The Bronx," Ellie said.

At the same moment both Michael and Manny said, "Which part?"

All three of them laughed.

Ellie pointed to her left, at the cars going north on the Deegan. "Up there," she said. "But how come you two get to ask all the questions?"

"We don't," Manny said. "Your turn. And don't worry, I'm like Radio Shack, if you've got questions, I've got answers."

Ellie said, "I have no idea what you're talking about."

"Join the club," Michael said.

"Okay," Ellie said, "I'll keep it simple: Who are you guys?"

Manny then tried to tell her both his and Michael's life stories in the space of about five minutes. What his father did, where he lived, where they went to school. How Michael and Carlos and Papi had come over on the boat.

Everything except what had happened to Papi.

When he finally stopped, just to take a breath, Ellie said to Michael, "You're Cuban? Really?"

"Cuban American now," he said. "That's what I'm taught to say." He tilted his head at her. "Where are you from?"

The mystery look again. Same small smile.

"Oh, I'm from the Caribbean, too," she said.

"Ellie Garcia," Manny said. "From somewhere in the Bronx and somewhere in the Caribbean before that. The girl who shows up out of nowhere to throw like a boy."

"And you, Mr. Manny Cabrera, talk more than any of my girlfriends," she said.

Michael laughed too loudly at that one. Manny gave him his shut-up look.

Michael asked Ellie if she could hang around for a while.

"Does that mean you're asking me to play?" she said.

He said, yeah, he guessed he was.

Then Michael said, "I can't tell who's the cat here and who's the little mouse . . . "

"You're the cat," Ellie said. "Like one my father used to sing to me about when I was little. Misifuz the cat."

Michael couldn't believe his ears. "*My* father used to sing me the same song!" he said. " '*Misifuz dormido en su cama está.*' "

"Misifuz the cat is sleeping on the bed," she said.

Michael said, "I thought it was just a Cuban song."

"My father told me it was *our* song," she said.

They both knew about Misifuz.

Cool, he thought.

She reached into his glove, took the ball out, smiled at him one last time, again looking to Michael like there was some joke she wouldn't let him in on.

"I'll pitch," she said.

And Michael said he'd catch for a change.

"A left-handed catcher?" Ellie said.

"As much as it physically pains me to admit this, he's not just the best pitcher on our team, he's the best catcher, too," Manny said. "And the best center fielder and . . ."

"Enough," Michael said.

Ellie said to Manny, "But I thought you were the catcher."

"Only because he's the best pitcher and the best center fielder," Manny said.

"Please shut up and hit," Michael said.

They agreed that everybody would get ten hits, then they'd go pick up whatever balls were scattered around the field before somebody else took a turn at bat.

The problem for Manny was getting his bat on the ball ten times.

He hit a few of Ellie's pitches at the start, when she wasn't throwing her hardest. But when she turned up the heat, the way Michael did when he got loose, Manny started to miss. Badly.

Finally he dribbled one to where the second baseman would have been, which made nine hits for him.

"Okay," Michael said to his friend. "Two outs, bottom of the ninth, runners on second and third, our team down by a run. Base hit sends us to Williamsport."

"There's an open base," Manny said. "If she knows what's good for her, she'll walk me."

"Bases loaded then, smart guy. No place to put you."

"Does that mean I can pitch from a full windup?" Ellie said.

Manny whistled through his teeth, the way he did when he was impressed by something. "She's good," he said.

Michael said, "An ice cream says you don't put the ball in play."

"Make it both our dinners at McDonald's. We were going there, anyway. You okay with that?"

"I'm good," Michael said, "Carlos gave me money."

"It's on then."

Manny fixed his helmet, dug in the way he did with his back foot, the one closest to Michael, wiggled his bat back and forth.

Ellie threw one past him, down the middle, a blazer, for strike one.

As Michael threw the ball back, Manny said, "Good hitters swing and miss sometimes on a pitch they like, so the pitcher will throw it again."

"I never heard that one," Michael said.

Ellie threw strike two past him. Same place, maybe a little closer to the outside corner.

"That pitch you wanted her to throw again?" Michael said, trying not to grin. "I think she just threw it."

Manny kept his eyes on the girl. "Shut up," he said to Michael.

"But," Michael said, ignoring him, "if I'm following your thinking here, you've got her right where you want her."

Manny wiggled his bat harder, his face suddenly serious, as if this were a real game, real bottom of the ninth, the field full of players instead of just the three of them on an afternoon Michael suddenly wanted to last forever.

Now Michael watched as Ellie went into the same high-kick windup Michael used—was she trying to copy him?—and threw a total screamer, a smoke alarm, past Manny Cabrera for strike three.

When the ball was in Michael's glove, he looked out at her. She hadn't even changed expression. Or maybe she was just trying to keep a straight face. She didn't say anything and neither did he and neither did Manny. Michael hadn't even moved his glove yet.

Of course Manny spoke first.

He dropped his bat, turned to Michael, and in a little-boy voice said, "I could use a hug."

They all laughed again.

Ellie had a good laugh, Michael noticed. She wasn't shy when she laughed, or embarrassed. Just happy.

When they stopped, Ellie said to Michael, "I haven't had a chance to hit against you yet."

"I've already thrown enough today," he said. "And, besides, we've got a game tomorrow."

Ellie put a hand on her hip, tilted her head a little, gave him a suspicious look. "Afraid a girl might get a hit off you?" she said.

"No," he said. "I'm never afraid somebody might get a hit."

"Is that bragging?"

"No, no, no," Michael said. Blushing again, he knew. "I just mean that putting your best up against somebody else's, that's not something that should make you afraid. That's the fun of it all."

He wanted to explain to this girl he'd just met that there were plenty of things that made him afraid, just not baseball.

Baseball always made him happy.

Never happier than today, he thought.

"And if I did pitch to you, and let you get a hit, you'd know it," Michael said.

"How do you know that?" Ellie said.

"Because you're just like me," Michael said.

They were sitting in the grass, a few yards from home plate. Manny had gone to get his cell phone out of his bat bag, saying he had to call his mom. Ellie said she had to go soon. Michael asked, "Where?"

Ellie answered, "No more questions for today."

As she said it, Michael saw that her eyes were focused on the area behind home plate, on the other side of the screen. “Who’s that with Manny?” she asked.

“Who’s *who* with Manny?” Michael asked in return.

“The policeman and the other man,” she said.

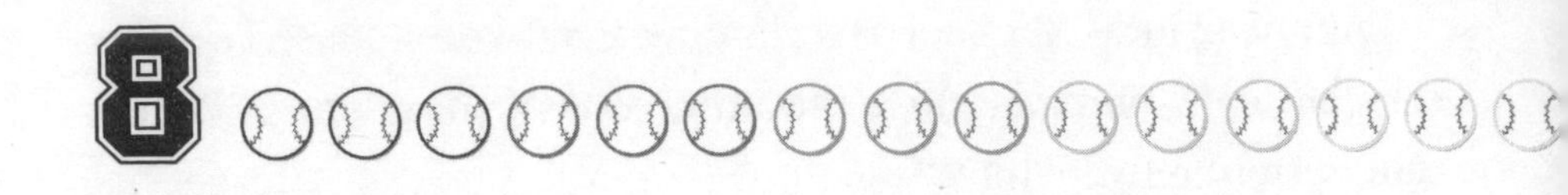

8

MICHAEL RECOGNIZED THE POLICEMAN WHO HAD HANDCUFFED THE PURSE stealer after Michael had hit him with the longest knockdown pitch ever, put the guy down not too far from where he and Ellie were sitting right now.

The other man wore a white shirt and a tie, even in the heat, carrying his jacket over his arm. He was smiling at Manny, then nodding, then laughing at something Manny said. Then lifting his chin and nodding in Michael's direction.

"Do you know them?" Ellie said.

"The policeman I do. Officer Crandall is his name. Officer Mark Crandall. I met him the other day."

"And who's that with him?" She was trying to angle her body to get a better look, because the policeman had moved now and was blocking her view.

"An Official Person," Michael said, knowing he was talking in capital letters.

"How can you tell?" Ellie grinned. "Officially, I mean."

"I just can."

Now he saw the Official Person giving Manny a friendly shove in their direction, the kind the coach gives you when he tells you to go get in the game. Manny jogged toward the outfield while Officer Crandall and his friend sat down on the home team's bench, on the first-base side of the field.

Michael got up now. So did Ellie.

When Manny was about twenty yards away, Michael couldn't wait any longer. "Who is that?" he said.

Ellie had moved a few steps closer to home plate, squinting into the sun at the two men. Before Manny could answer, she said, "He works for the Bronx borough president, Mr. Amorosa. I forget his exact job."

Manny said, "He works in public relations for Mr. Amorosa. He says his name is Mr. Lima." He stared at Ellie. "But how do you know him?"

Michael thought Ellie seemed nervous all of a sudden, even though he had no idea what she had to be nervous about. "I met him one time," she said. "With my dad."

"Anyway," Manny said to Michael, "he wants to meet you, is all. It turns out Officer Crandall said something to one of his superiors about what you did with Ramon—that was the thief's name, Ramon—and the superior said something, and it somehow ended up in Mr. Amorosa's office. Mr. Lima says they want you . . . and your parents . . . to come down and have your picture taken with Mr. Amorosa. People hear so much about crime in the South Bronx, he said, they want to play up their twelve-year-old crimestopper."

Michael felt himself looking all around Macombs Dam Park now, all corners of the green grass, everywhere except at the two men on the home team's bench.

He was never, under any conditions, supposed to talk to any Official Person without Carlos. The only reason that he had talked to Officer Crandall that day was because he had no choice. He had been afraid that if he ran off when he saw a policeman coming, he would look as guilty as that Ramon guy.

"What did you tell him?" Michael said. "Mr. Lima, I mean."

"You see him laughing before?" Manny said. "I tried to make a joke of it. I told them they were talking to your agent, and that I'd have to clear it with you first. That's when Mr. Lima told me to go clear it already."

Manny turned now, put on his biggest smile, waved at the two men, held up a finger. One more moment, please.

From behind them, Michael heard Ellie say, "I've got to go." He turned his head and saw her running toward Ruppert Place, the same as she had the first day.

"Wait!" he yelled at her back.

But she kept running, around the end of the basketball court, up the hill, toward the flow of people heading for the gates at Yankee Stadium.

She held up her hand in some kind of wave without breaking stride.

Michael looked at her, looked back at Officer Crandall and Mr. Lima, said to Manny, "Wait for me at McDonald's."

He ran after her.

"Michael, wait!" Manny said. "What the heck am I going to tell them?"

Over his shoulder, glove in his right hand, one ball still in the pocket, chasing after the baseball girl, one who seemed to have secrets of her own, Michael smiled, even as scared as he was.

"Tell them the truth," he shouted at Manny. "Tell them this is the first day of my whole life that I started chasing girls."

Only when he looked up the hill, she was gone.

Again.

There was another policeman right in front of Michael as he came racing up the hill, on this street where he always imagined his baseball world ended and the Yankees' began.

He wanted to ask the man if he had seen a pretty girl with a baseball glove under her arm.

Then he stopped to catch his breath, imagining how a scene like that would play itself out. What was he going to ask this policeman, had he seen a girl with a baseball glove outside the Stadium before a home game?

The man would probably look at him and say, "I've seen about fifty, would you care to narrow it down a little bit?"

Michael knew there was no point in even looking for Ellie up here. Or asking anybody for help. Or trying to explain why this friend of his, a girl friend, was running away from him in the first place.

So he slowed down now and walked right past the policeman, who seemed to be guarding the Stadium Club entrance to the Stadium. When he got to the corner of 161st and Ruppert, he stopped to look back on the field at Macombs Dam Park, saw Manny in the distance, walking away from the Little League field with Officer Crandall on one side of him and Mr. Lima on the other.

Michael could see Manny chattering away, talking with his mouth and his hands at the same time, in a way that always made Michael wonder if the hands were trying to keep up with the mouth, or if it was the other way around. He saw Manny look up at one man, then the other, then saw both men start to laugh.

Manny the Entertainer. Like that guy Cedric the Entertainer in the movies.

It had been such a perfect day, Michael thought to himself. Him and Manny and Ellie Garcia, laughing and playing ball and inventing games and being happy to be on the field, and with each other. A perfect summer day when it was as if Michael could hypnotize himself, make himself believe that everything was going to work out right, that the Clippers would make it to Williamsport, that he and Carlos wouldn't be found out before Carlos turned eighteen.

That he and his brother would always be together.

Except now an Official Person had come to his field, which in the summer was as much his home as 825 Gerard.

What was he going to do the next time this Mr. Lima came around?

Michael felt himself shiver, even though the heat of the day had carried over into early evening, to when the Yankee game was set to begin.

They knew where to find him now.

It was Carlos's regular night off from Hector's, so he and Michael and Manny were chowing down on all the food Manny and Michael had brought from McDonald's, listening to the Yankee game on the radio.

Actually, Michael was doing most of the listening while Manny caught Carlos up on what had happened at the field. As always, Manny made himself out to be the hero of everything. It was another part of their deal, except on the ballfield. Once they got to the ballfield, Manny was always content, or so it seemed to Michael, to play the part of sidekick.

"They definitely asked you for Michael's last name?" Carlos asked Manny.

"I thought about giving them a middle name or something, just to throw them off for now," Manny said, his mouth full of fries. "But if they found out later that I'd lied about something that easy to find out, I figured they'd be asking themselves why I lied about something that easy to find out."

"But they didn't ask you for an address?" Carlos said.

"Nah," Manny said.

He looked at Michael across the table. "You gonna finish your fries?" he said. Michael shook his head. Manny grabbed a handful, said, "I think they were probably about to ask me where, but it was right then that my boy here decided to run after his new sweetie."

"I was running away from them," Michael said. "And she is not my sweetie, dorkball."

Michael got up and walked over to where the radio sat on the coffee table, wanting to hear better, and not wanting to have Manny catch him blushing. Again.

Top of the third for the Orioles, runners on second and third against El Grande.

Two outs.

Manny wouldn't let up, of course. "You told me you were running after her, remember?" Manny said.

"Shhhhh," Michael said.

Then listened as John Sterling, the Yankee announcer, his voice excited, said "Heeeeeee struck out him out," and El Grande was out of the inning.

At least somebody was winning something today.

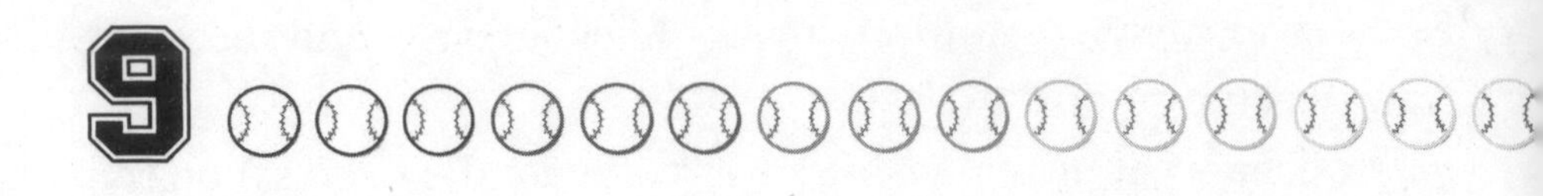

THEY HAD DRIVEN UP TO NEW ROCHELLE TO PLAY WESTCHESTER SOUTH—the team they all thought of as the Justins now—in the old blue bus from the small bus company near the Third Avenue Bridge that Mr. Minaya managed, in what he called his day job.

Manny joked with Mr. Minaya that the shock absorbers from this particular bus seemed to have turned into shock producers, but the kids loved the old bus, anyway, loved the idea of any kind of road trip out of the Bronx, just because it made them feel big.

The field in New Rochelle turned out to be beautiful, the infield and outfield grass looking as if they were being cared for by big-league groundskeepers like Kel's dad. Even the infield dirt had been raked before they got there. There were colorful ads for local stores on outfield walls that looked pretty close to Michael—pitchers always noticed—and a concessions truck set up in the parking lot behind home plate, and even new-looking bleachers on both sides of the field, for the home team and the visitors, not that the Clippers ever had many parents who made road trips.

Michael even noticed what looked like a small green press box set up on the Westchester South side of the field, even though he couldn't imagine what kind of press would want to be covering their game. Maybe the public address announcer sat up there; they had heard somebody testing a microphone, a voice coming from unseen speakers, when they had filed out of the bus.

When he heard the voice coming from the speakers, Manny immediately turned himself into the Yankees' PA announcer, the one who sounded like the voice of God. "Now coming in to pitch for the

Clippers," Manny said, making his voice even deeper than Anthony's. "Michael Arroyo. Number thirty-three." Pause. "Arroyo."

Michael said, "I'm not sure that's exactly how he does it, the Yankee guy."

"Close enough," Manny said.

Michael said, "I still think it needs work."

"I sound exactly like him and you know it," Manny said. "Jealousy does not become you, Star. I'm just telling you that as a friend."

"I try to keep it under control," Michael said.

Justin the Jerk started for Westchester South.

As far as Michael and the guys could tell, he spent more time before the game staring Michael down than warming up.

After they had finished taking infield and outfield practice and were back at their bench, Anthony Fierro came up to Michael. Anthony could be just as funny as Manny, he just didn't try as hard.

Or as often.

"Blondie Boy seems to think this is the finals of the Olympic Staredown event," Anthony said.

Anthony was about the same shape as Justin. A little shorter than Michael, but heavier, and solid. One time in a game, there had been a grounder to Anthony at first, and Michael thought he had to get off the mound and cover first base. Only at the last second, Anthony decided to sprint for the base himself. They arrived at the same moment, Michael couldn't get out of the way, and the two of them collided.

Michael ended up about halfway to the home team's bench at Macombs. The star, Manny had said to him later, seeing stars.

Anthony, Michael knew, wasn't afraid of anybody or anything.

"That guy's a punk, you can just see it," he said.

"All I did was strike him out," Michael said.

Kel said, "Seems like the boy's still got some issues going for him on that there."

Justin was staring at them from the mound now, while his team took infield practice. Kel stepped forward, gave the kid what he called his "buggy look," eyes all wide. Giving a little shake to his head as he did.

"Kel," Michael said. "You've got to lead off tonight, and he's got the ball."

Manny said, "Yeah, but you've got it later."

They went and sat down next to Manny on the bench, giving him room, because he was doing what he did before every game, neatly laying out his equipment. Mask. Chest protector. Shin guards. Manny called them his instruments.

Anthony nodded at his instruments now. "You know what they really call a catcher's stuff?"

Manny was fiddling with the straps on his shin guards. "What?"

"The tools of ignorance," Anthony said, then put his hand up, as if inviting high fives from the group.

"I'm not even dignifying your ignorance with a comment," Manny said. "*You're* a tool of ignorance."

That got a laugh out of everybody.

From the mound, they heard old Justin say, "What's so funny?"

Manny, who couldn't keep a thought inside his head sometimes, said, "You are, Skippy."

The guy bit. "My name's not Skippy."

Kel stood up, stared out at him. "But you look exactly like a Skippy, no lie."

"Why don't you come out here and say that?" Justin said, gesturing with what looked like a pretty expensive glove.

Anthony stood up now, stepped in front of Kel. "Hey, dude, why don't you take a chill pill?"

Then Mr. Minaya appeared, as if out of nowhere, and shooed them all back on the bench, reminding them about the team rule: No trash talk.

Ever.

Under any circumstances.

No matter how much trash the other side was talking at them.

"Now quiet down," he said.

As usual, Manny thought "quiet down" applied to everybody on the team except him.

"Well, as my mom likes to say," he said, "this should certainly be a festive occasion."

Little did they know.

10

It was the top of the fourth inning.

Manny pointed to Justin.

"He may be as pretty as Brad Pitt," Manny said. "But the boy can pitch."

"Like, mad pitch," Kel said, Justin having struck him out twice now.

Michael was used to the way Kel talked by now, and how his cool way of talking seemed to influence the other guys on the team, and Maria, too. So "mad" with him was a way of amping up whatever word came next. Maria was mad good-looking. Michael had, like, a mad arm. Chris Rock, who Michael only got to see in the movies, never on television, was mad funny.

Like that.

"Before," Anthony Fierro said now, "we thought the guy was just mad, period."

"Dude," Kel said, using another one of his favorite words, one he could make into a question, an exclamation point, show surprise with, anger, anything. Sometimes, like now, he used it to end the conversation, as if saying, case closed on old Justin.

Michael didn't need to look at the scorebook to know that he was the only one on the Clippers Justin hadn't struck out yet. Michael was batting third today. Justin had come up and in on him his first time up, knocking Michael back off the plate and then glaring at him again afterward. But Michael had gotten back into the left-handers' side of the batter's box, dug back in, and promptly taken a low, outside pitch over the third baseman's head and into the left-field corner of the cool ballpark, the ball rolling all the way to a Home Depot sign out there.

As Michael came flying around second, he saw their left fielder having trouble picking the ball up and just kept motoring into third, cap flying off his head.

Stand-up triple.

"Are you always this lucky?" Justin said when he got the ball back.

Michael ignored him. Thinking: I've never talked to a base runner in my life. Instead he turned to Mr. Minaya, who was coaching third. But Justin was still talking. Now Michael heard him say, "Great job out there!" Michael wondered what that meant until he turned back around and saw Justin pointing to his left fielder. Yelling at him in front of everybody for the crime of giving Michael an extra base.

The kid out there just got into his ready defensive position, like he was studying the grass at his feet for some kind of test later.

On the first pitch to Anthony, who was up next, Justin tried to throw the ball about two hundred miles per hour, and bounced the ball in front of his catcher, who had absolutely no chance to even block the ball. It rolled all the way to the backstop and Michael could have walked home—backward—with the Clippers' first run of the game.

This time when Justin the Jerk got the ball back he snapped at his catcher, "Get in front of the stupid ball."

To the catcher's credit, he said, "With what, the snack truck?"

Their coach stepped right out on that one and waggled his finger at the catcher. Not Justin. "Hey, Brendan," the coach said. "Just catch."

Manny said, "That's not just any coach. That's Justin's old man, I guarantee it."

Westchester South tied it off Anthony in the bottom of the fourth. Justin doubled with two outs, and later came around to score when Anthony walked the next three hitters. Then the same thing happened to Justin in the top of the fifth: He started walking guys all over the place. "He's lost the strike zone," Manny said on the bench, using one of Mr. Minaya's favorite expressions. Losing the strike zone. It made Michael smile, the way a lot of old-time baseball expressions did. Sometimes he imagined a whole team on their hands and knees, searching for the strike zone the way the Clippers did one time when Anthony lost one of his contact lenses.

It began when Justin walked Maria on four pitches even though she hadn't made contact with the ball the whole game. A girl. They were afraid on the bench it would make Justin's head explode. So it was no surprise when he walked the next hitter, Kel, on five pitches.

Then, with Justin's face getting redder and redder with each ball out of the strike zone, even whining to the umpire a couple of times on pitches that weren't even close, he walked Manny to load the bases.

Michael was up again.

The count went to three-and-oh, all three of the pitches high and wide. Brendan, the catcher, Michael could see out of the corner of his eye, twice had to make diving backhand catches to keep Maria at third base.

The coach, who they were sure now was Justin's dad, stood up in front of their bench.

"Just relax and throw strikes," he said.

Michael stepped out and smiled, he couldn't help himself. It was always the dumbest thing he heard from any coach in any game. Relax and throw strikes. Right. He'd look out and see some eleven- or twelve-year-old pitcher about to squeeze the seams off the ball, about to start crying because he couldn't throw a strike to save his life, and the coach would think the perfect thing to say was, Relax.

Throw strikes.

Justin thought Michael was laughing at him.

"You think this is funny?" Justin yelled in at him.

"Huh?" Michael said.

"Just pitch, son," the umpire said.

"He's laughing at me," Justin said.

"No I'm not," Michael said.

The ump said, "Play ball."

Justin went into his full windup and threw a fastball that hit Michael in the head.

The first thing Michael saw when he opened his eyes was the worried face of Manny Cabrera, close enough to Michael that he could smell the Orbit Bubblemint gum his friend was constantly chomping on.

"I know you think this is what heaven will look like," Manny said. "But you're not dead."

Mr. Minaya was crouched next to Manny. Standing behind them, Michael could see Kel, Maria, Anthony. Chris Nourse, their third baseman.

He sat up now. Mr. Minaya said, "Slowly."

Michael said, "I'm okay."

"Okay then," Mr. Minaya said.

Michael realized his helmet was gone. "Where'd it get me?" he said, because he honestly couldn't remember. He just remembered the ball coming for his eyeballs, turning away, hearing the ball on his helmet, hitting the deck.

Manny said, "Tip of the helmet."

"The bill," Mr. Minaya said.

"Check it out," Manny said.

He held up Michael's batting helmet for him to see. The bill was all crooked now, as if one of the wheels of their old bus had rolled over it.

Mr. Minaya said, "How's the head?"

Manny said, "Hard," obviously convinced that everything was going to be all right now that Michael was up and talking.

"It doesn't hurt, actually," Michael said.

"I can't believe they didn't throw that puss out of the game," Manny said.

Mr. Minaya said, "His dad pointed out that since he couldn't hit the catcher's glove when he wanted to, how could he hit Michael's head."

"But he thought Michael was laughing at him," Manny said.

"Hush," Mr. Minaya said.

Miraculously, Manny did.

Now Mr. Minaya said, "Mike, I'm gonna take you out."

"No!" Michael said.

It came out of him with more force than he intended.

Mr. Minaya put a hand on his shoulder. "I know what a gamer you are," he said. "But you just took the hardest fastball I've seen this season—next to yours—in the coconut."

"Helmet," Michael said.

The truth was, his head did hurt, but only around his forehead, where the helmet must have scraped him as Justin's high hard one had twisted it around. "Please let me stay in," Michael said.

"Hey guys," they all heard now.

Michael turned and saw the umpire standing over him. He didn't look much older than Carlos, but he had been doing a good job calling balls and strikes, and hustling down to first when there was a ground ball, since he was working alone. Some of the umps they ran into acted as if they didn't want to be there, as if they were just going through the motions until they got paid and got out of there.

This ump, Michael could see, cared about the game, doing things right. Michael always picked up on it right away, a passion for baseball, like they were wearing a sign.

The ump hunched down next to him. "You okay?"

"Yes sir."

"Is he staying in?" To Mr. Minaya.

Mr. Minaya looked at Michael, then at the umpire. "He is."

Manny helped Michael to his feet. The Westchester South parents clapped. Maria, who had scored on the play, handed Michael her batting helmet, since in Little League you had to wear a helmet on the bases.

Justin, soft-tossing with his third baseman to stay warm, didn't even turn around.

"Please, pretty please, tell me that punk is going down," Manny said, his voice low.

"Oh, he's going down," Michael said, and jogged down to first base.

He missed with his first two pitches of the bottom of the sixth, the Clippers still holding on to their 2–1 lead. Maybe I'm having a delayed reaction, he thought, going behind the mound to rub up a baseball they'd been using for three innings. He had been beaned. He could never understand that expression, either. Did that mean your head was a bean? Or the ball? Even now, following the twists and turns of English made him feel like he was trying to read one of those subway maps they had on the walls of the trains. . . .

Now all his teammates cared about was if he was going to bean Justin or not.

Manny had just come out to remind him Justin was up third in the inning.

"Go," Michael said. "Catch."

"Go, Manny," Manny said. "Sit, Manny. You ever notice you talk to me like a dog sometimes?"

When Manny got halfway back to the plate, Michael couldn't help it. "Good boy," he said. Then he threw three straight blazers. The guy swung and missed at all of them. One out.

Three more to the second guy. The kid, a black kid who seemed to be smiling the whole game, whether things were going good for his team or not, was walking back to the bench before the ump even called strike three.

Two outs.

Justin now.

Manny called time. Anthony came in from first, Kel from short, Chris Nourse from third. Maria stayed at second, saying to Michael, "You guys just do your guy thing, I'm fine here."

Manny said, "You owe the sucker one."

Kel said, "Check it out: You could hit the next three of those suckers and still win the game."

Anthony, who never came to the mound, mostly because he didn't need to when Michael was pitching, took off his cap, rubbed a hand over his new buzz cut, and grinned. "Buzz him," he said.

The ump, Michael saw, had come out in front of the plate to stand with his hands on his hips. "How's about we save the rest of this for instant-messaging later?"

They all left.

The ump turned and walked back to the plate. As he did, Michael saw Mr. Minaya get up off the bench and take a few steps toward the field, as if he knew what they had all been talking about on the mound. Michael looked over and Mr. Minaya gave him a look that said, Don't.

Michael got ready to pitch. Justin did his big-leaguer pose, fiddling with his two batting gloves, motioning with his right hand for the umpire to wait while he dug in. When he was ready, he finally looked out at Michael.

He's scared, Michael thought.

He would never say this out loud, but he knew exactly why Justin was scared.

Because as hard as he throws, I throw harder.

Michael went into his high-kick windup, ducked his head behind his glove, brought his arm forward as hard as he ever had.

And threw the only curveball he was going to throw all season.

And not just any curve. Michael threw the kind of big, slow hook that El Grande would throw sometimes, one that seemed to float out of the sky like a Frisbee, one that the radar gun would clock at fifty miles an hour sometimes.

Justin was a left-handed hitter, too. As easy as Michael threw the ball, all Justin saw was the ball coming for his fat head, which is why he fell away from it, bat flying out of his hands, as if Michael were trying to drill a hole through his helmet.

Except that as the ball started to lose altitude, it also started to break, breaking down, spinning right into Manny's mitt about belt high as the umpire held up his right hand and yelled, "Stee-rike!"

The Clippers did nothing. Not even Manny, who seemed speechless for the first time in his life. It was Justin's teammates who laughed at how silly Michael had made him look. When Justin got back up, Michael could see the back of his uniform full of dirt. He glared at his own bench now, quickly got back into the batter's box, looking as if he wanted to hit the next pitch into the parking lot. "Go ahead," he said to Michael, "throw that junk again, see what happens."

Michael shook his head, like he was shaking off Manny. "Nah," he said.

Manny put down one finger and Michael threw a fastball past Justin, who took a violent cut and missed. Then Michael did it again.

Strike three.

Game over.

After Michael had gotten high fives from his teammates in back of the mound, he turned around to see Justin still standing at home plate.

"How old are you, really?" he called out.

Michael just stared.

"Don't you understand English?" Justin said. "I asked you a question."

"I'm twelve," Michael said, knowing as he did he shouldn't have been talking to the guy.

Justin wouldn't let it go.

"What'd you do, drop a couple of years on the boat over, like you guys do?"

Manny stepped in now.

"Dude," he said, "you're lucky you didn't drop a little something there on strike one."

Justin walked away then, as if he wasn't paying any attention, waving them off, not looking back.

Michael watched him go.

Wondering how a kid from Westchester knew anything about his boat ride over.

And why he even stinking cared?

11

Mr. Lima, from the Bronx borough president's office, the man from the park, in his white shirt and tie, was in front of 825 Gerard when Mr. Minaya dropped Michael off after the Westchester South game.

Mrs. C was with him.

She was sitting in the lawn chair she would set up on the sidewalk sometimes, on warm summer nights like this. Sometimes some of the older people in the building would be there with her, with chairs of their own or just sitting on the front steps, listening to music on a battery-powered radio one of them would bring with them. Or somebody would open one of the front windows, in one of the first-floor apartments facing the street, and they would listen to one of the Spanish-music stations. Unless the men would win out and there would be a Yankee game on. Sometimes, if the game was on, Michael would come down and sit with them, imagining that the residents of 825 Gerard were one big family, with Mrs. Cora the grandma of them all.

Mostly the old people would just talk, in English and Spanish, like they were making two languages into one, and watch the world go by.

Michael wanted it to go by 825 Gerard right now.

He felt his heart racing inside him as if he'd just gone from first to third on a single. Or as if he'd run all the way here from New Rochelle.

Maybe getting hit in the head wasn't going to be the worst thing that happened to him tonight.

Usually Mrs. C didn't get out of her lawn chair until she was ready to go to bed. She would joke that picking herself up was even harder at the end of the day than walking up the hill from River Avenue. But she got right up out of her chair now, no problem, popped up like one of those little pop-up messages he'd see at Manny's when Manny would make him watch a music video on MTV, greeted Michael like he really was her grandson.

Her long-lost grandson.

Mrs. C hugged him to her so fiercely, Michael had trouble breathing for a second, kissed the side of his head, and whispered, "Say as little as possible, little one."

Then she pulled back and plopped back down in her chair as Mr. Lima came over and put out his hand.

"Fred Lima, son," he said. "Press secretary for Mr. Amorosa, the borough president for these parts."

Making the Bronx sound a little bit like the Old West or something.

Michael shook the man's hand the way Papi had taught him, firmly, looking him right in the eye.

"Michael Arroyo," he said.

"Finally I get to meet the boy hero," Mr. Lima said.

Manny always said that the only player on the team who never got nervous was Michael.

Except now.

"I just got lucky, is all," he said.

He looked up Gerard, to where some kids were playing catch with a football, and imagined himself sprinting past them, away, the way he'd sprinted away from Mr. Lima the other night.

"Not what I hear," Mr. Lima said. "I hear that the only twelve-year-old who could have made that throw is the twelve-year-old who did."

Michael looked at Mrs. C. She said, "Just say thank you, little one."

"Thank you," he said, looking down.

Mr. Lima said, "Mrs. Cora here tells me that she's sort of been looking out for you and your brother while your dad's out of town."

Mrs. Cora jumped right in, not waiting for Michael to answer. "You should see the two of them eat my *paella,*" she said. She pointed at Michael. "But this one here," she said, "no matter how much he eats, he stays as skinny as one of my sewing needles."

Now no one said anything. From one of the high windows, Michael could hear the voices of the Yankee announcers. Where were they tonight? Detroit? Chicago?

Chicago. To play the White Sox.

Mr. Lima cleared his throat. "Well," he said, "I'm glad I finally tracked you down, Mr. Michael Arroyo. The other day I would have needed one of those little motor scooters the police use to ride around the Stadium to catch up with you."

Michael said, "I was running after my girlfriend."

Girlfriend? That came out a little too easily.

Mrs. Cora said, "My Michael has a new girlfriend?"

"She's a girl, and a friend, Mrs. C. Somebody I met in the park."

Then he yawned. It just came out of him, the way it did on the mound sometimes. Manny thought it just showed how super-relaxed he was, no matter how close the game. Michael knew better: The yawn meant he was feeling some nerves. He heard Tom Seaver on a Mets game one time say how he used to yawn in big spots and his teammates all thought he was crazy. It made him feel better, a little less crazy about his own yawning.

He covered it now by saying to Mr. Lima, "I'm kind of tired, sir. We had a tough game tonight, and I was going to head upstairs and listen to the Yankees–White Sox game until my brother comes home."

"Carlos," Mr. Lima said. "Going into his senior year of high school, right?"

Everybody knew everything all of a sudden.

Almost everything.

"Right," Michael said.

"Well," Mr. Lima said, "since I'd never want to keep a good Bronx boy from listening to his favorite team, let me tell you what I've been telling Mrs. Cora here, since she turns out to be the one whose purse you rescued: We'd like to have you and her and your brother and your father, if he gets back in the next couple of days, come down and have your picture taken with Mr. Amorosa. And Officer Crandall, of course."

Michael said, "Oh, you don't have to go to all that trouble."

"We want to, that's the thing," Mr. Lima said. "And it's no trouble, really. This is the kind of story, right from our neighborhoods, that people need to know about. A boy from the neighborhood coming to the aid of a woman like Mrs. Cora, one who turns out to be one of his best friends. In the process, the boy isn't just a friend to her, but to the police."

Mrs. C started to say something but Mr. Lima put up a hand, smiling. "Please, I promise this is the end of my speech," he said. "There's still too many people who only want to talk about crime in the Bronx, even though we're much safer now than we've ever been. We want to shine a spotlight on a crimestopper."

He handed Michael his business card. "Tell your dad about it when you talk to him," he said. "Will he be calling you tonight?"

"Probably not," Michael said, looking off.

He looked at the card. There was a business phone number,

a home phone number, a cell phone number, a fax number, an e-mail address.

"Or you can just have your dad call me directly," Mr. Lima said. "We'll set something up for next week maybe."

He leaned down, shook Mrs. Cora's hand, told her it was nice chatting with her, and not to get up.

"Don't worry," she said, "I won't."

Mr. Lima shook Michael's hand one more time, then said he was going to go jump on the next train and head home.

"Your father must be very proud of you," he said to Michael, and was gone.

For now.

"What are we going to do?" Michael said.

"Eat," Mrs. Cora said, extending her hand in a way that meant Michael needed to help her up this time. "I made pot roast."

"I meant . . . ," Michael said, folding up the lawn chair.

"I know what you meant, little one," she said. "And I said, let's go eat."

Mrs. C thought food could cure just about anything.

12

MANNY SUGGESTED THEY HIRE SOMEBODY TO PLAY THE PART OF Michael's dad.

Have the guy show up in a nice suit, Manny said, smile for the camera, say how proud he was of his little boy, and then they could all be done with it.

"Don't take this the wrong way," Michael said to him. "But you're insane."

They were in Michael's apartment in the middle of the afternoon, hanging out until the Clippers–Grand Concourse game at Macombs Dam Park. Manny had been coming up with one crazy plan after another even though Carlos had decided that they weren't going to do anything about Mr. Lima's invitation, at least not for the time being. If Mr. Lima called again, or stopped by, Carlos would say they were going to wait a few more days for their father, and if he wasn't back by next week, then they'd just have to come down to the borough president's office without him. For now their story was that their uncle had suffered a setback.

"I'm sure you understand, sir," Carlos had said, rehearsing the scene, pretending Michael was Mr. Lima. "Family has to come first."

Manny said they were just putting off the inevitable, that they should do it now and get it over with. He imagined the whole thing as a movie now, one he was making up as he went along, the kind where the kids got together and put one over on the adults.

The kind, Michael thought, that always had a happy ending.

"Work with me on this, Star," Manny said. "We could use one of the men who live in the building."

"Yeah," Michael said. "We'll get Mr. Chu, that ought to fool them."

"It's a good thing I'm the only one who sees the snippy side of you," Manny said.

He was still lying on the floor in front of the pillows they'd set up as goals in sock hockey. On his back, hands laced behind his head, eyes full of fun. Michael knew his game: If he acted as if he wasn't taking any of this too seriously then maybe Michael wouldn't worry as much.

"What about your super, Mr. Ruiz?" Manny said.

"What about him?"

"He's about the right age, he's dark like us. And," Manny said, "you seem to be the only person in the whole world he actually likes."

"Until Carlos can't come up with the rent money."

"You know my parents would help out if it ever came to that."

"You know the deal," Michael said. "Carlos and me don't want your parents to get involved. Your dad's with the fire department. It makes him an Official Person, even if he doesn't act like one. If he finds out there's no parent here, he's supposed to tell."

"He'd never tell in a million years, officially or unofficially," Manny said. "I'm getting hungry again, by the way."

"Huge surprise."

"First, back to my brilliant plan."

"No."

"We could get Mr. Ruiz to shave that ugly beard of his and that mustache, nobody'd recognize him when he's standing there like a proud papa."

Michael said, "If I let you finish the Oreos, will you drop this?"

"You didn't tell me there was a backup bag of Oreos."

"You didn't ask."

"Where?"

"Fridge. In the drawer where Carlos keeps the lettuce."

Manny rolled up into a sitting position, gave Michael what was supposed to be a mean look, disappeared into the kitchen. From in there Michael heard, "Somebody puts Oreos in with vegetables, it means they're hiding them."

He came in with a fistful of the greatest cookies ever invented and tossed one to Michael. "Back to my plan," he said.

Michael said, "We lie enough already, Man the Man. And that is no lie. Every time an adult says something, like, your father must be soooo proud, I feel like all they have to do is take one look at my face to know something's wrong."

"We just need to get through the season, Star, we both know that."

"Carlos keeps saying we will, but he never tells me what his plan is."

"He's probably afraid you'll shoot the sucker down like you do my plans," Manny said. "We need something to wash these down with." Back up, back into the kitchen, back with two glasses of milk. Sometimes Michael found himself wondering how many visits to 825 Gerard per week Manny would have to make before Carlos had to think about taking on a third job.

"You sure you've had enough snacks?" Michael said. "I wouldn't want your stomach to start growling about the fourth inning."

"Is that a dig? Are you saying I eat too much?"

"Never," Michael said. He drank down all of his milk and said, "You ready to go play baseball?"

"I can't believe you even have to ask," Manny said.

Maybe Ellie would be there today, Michael thought. Even with everything else on his mind, he never went too long these days without thinking about the pretty girl, the mystery girl, with the long legs.

Sometimes he wondered what her secrets were.

Grand Concourse was their second-to-last game before the play-offs. The Clippers had played them the very first week of the season, but Grand Concourse—their team nickname was the Pinstripers, in honor of the Yankees—didn't have three of their best kids that day, because they'd come down with some kind of stomach virus. Michael had started that game, but it was 12–0 for the Clippers after two innings and 14–0 in the fourth, at which point the slaughter rule had gone into effect. Game over.

But the Pinstripers, they knew, had become a good team after that, and were now in fourth place in District 22.

"They're going to have a little something to prove," Mr. Minaya said during batting practice. "So we're going to need our 'A game' if we want to stay in first."

Mr. Minaya talked about their "A game" a lot. Another one of his favorite expressions.

Now Manny said to Mr. Minaya, "You sure you don't think B-plus will do the job tonight?"

Before Mr. Minaya could answer, Kel said, "This close to the play-offs, when we might have to play their sorry butts again, I'm not sure we should show them our 'A' game, or even our 'B' game."

Michael smiled. "I see what Kel means, Mr. M."

Manny said, "Coach, you think Michael's saying we only need our 'C' game? Wow, I hope he's not taking them lightly."

Anthony Fierro sang, "Now we've said our ABC's . . ."

Mr. Minaya walked away, shaking his head, saying, "We've all obviously spent too much time together."

"No worries, Coach," Manny called after him. "We always give you an 'A' for effort."

"Just play hard," their coach said. "And . . ."

Together, Michael and Kel and Manny and Anthony yelled, "Have fun!"

Michael struck out the side in the top of the first, three up, three down, eleven pitches. He also hit his first over-the-fence home run of the season, a two-run job in the bottom of the first. It looked like they might be on their way to another slaughter-rule win when they scored five more runs after that, to make it 7–0. At that point Mr. Minaya announced he was going to let Michael pitch one more inning, and then was going to let Maria pitch for the first time all season.

Michael saw Ellie after he struck out the first two Pinstripers in the top of the second.

She was sitting on the hill beyond the basketball courts, by herself, as usual. He'd heard somebody on the bench say it was five minutes to seven, which meant the Yankee game was about to start. They were back from their road trip, El Grande scheduled to start against the Minnesota Twins, a team he'd nearly no-hit the other time he'd faced them this season, back in June.

Michael got two fast strikes on what was going to be his last batter of the night, unless the guy got on. Which Michael knew he wasn't going to do, not the way he felt tonight, one of those nights when he felt as if he could pitch this way for all six innings without even breaking a sweat.

One strike to go now.

For Ellie's benefit, nobody else's, he kicked his right leg even higher than usual, El Grande high, really doing it up.

But he must have moved slightly on the rubber, to where the

Pinstripers' pitcher had been pushing off into the dirt, and his left toe got stuck in a small hole there. And because of his high kick, he lost his balance.

And proceeded to fall right on his butt.

The ball still in his left hand.

Even the batter knew it was all right to step out of the box and laugh, because all of Michael's teammates, and Mr. Minaya, were doing the exact same thing.

Sitting there next to the mound, Michael couldn't help it.

He laughed, too.

Manny called time and came walking out to the mound. Michael was still down. Manny looked down at him and said, "I'm not sure what the degree of difficulty was, but you sure as heck stuck the landing."

Michael stood up, cleaned himself off as best he could, got back on the mound, and immediately looked past the basketball courts. He wanted Ellie to still be there, because he planned to hustle over there as soon as the half inning was over. At the same time, though, he hoped she had missed his clown show.

She hadn't.

It was as if she had been waiting patiently for him to look over at her. As if she knew he would. As if they really did have some kind of mental telepathy going. Because as soon as he looked at her, she went into an exaggerated high-kick motion of her own, a perfect right-hander's impression of what he'd just tried to do.

Then she was the clown show, only on purpose, staggering into a fall, rolling down the hill.

When she got to the bottom, she stood up, put her hands above her head, and applauded him. Michael could see she was laughing, too.

He shook his head as if shaking off one of Manny's signs and got back on the mound. He went with a shorter kick this time, then burned one in for strike three. When he looked past the basketball courts to see if Ellie had seen that one, she was gone.

Or maybe just hiding.

Michael thought about going over to look for her, then decided he would stay on the bench for the rest of the game, be a good teammate and cheer his team on even if he wasn't playing. So he did. Every once in a while he would remember Ellie tumbling down the hill, and smile.

One of these nights, he thought, they were going to have a lot to talk about, if she'd ever hang around long enough.

The Clippers ended up winning, 10–6. Maria gave up some runs, and they hit a few balls hard off her, but she did pretty well, pitching better than some of the guys Mr. Minaya had thrown in there during the season in blowout games, just to give them a chance. They all went rushing out to the mound after the final out, as if she were the one who'd won a World Series game, then got into the line to shake hands with the Pinstripers.

"You guys are only acting this excited because I'm a girl," she said.

"No way," Manny said. "You pitched great."

"Said a girly boy," Kel said.

Manny said, "I heard that."

It was right after that when Mr. Gibbs, the Grand Concourse coach, came over to Mr. Minaya and asked if he could have a word with him. Michael watched the two men walk down the right-field line. They stayed out there a long time, Mr. Gibbs doing most of the talking. And whatever he was saying, Michael could see that Mr. M didn't like it very much, because he kept shaking his head, taking his cap off, and rubbing his forehead hard, the way he would when something went wrong for the Clippers during a game.

When he came back to the bench, Michael asked him if something had happened during the game to make Mr. Gibbs mad.

"I wish," Mr. M said. "But it's a little more serious than that."

Then he told Michael that there had been an official complaint made by the Westchester South team, demanding that the Clippers produce Michael's birth certificate.

"But I gave you the envelope my father gave me," Michael said, knowing he had given it to Mr. M only days before Papi had died.

"You did," Mr. M said. "Just not one with your birth certificate inside."

Mr. Gibbs found out when he had somebody at the league office pull Michael's file. And what they'd come up with was the baptism certificate that the commissioners would sometimes accept for foreign-born players.

"If they'd asked me, I could have saved them the trouble of checking," Mr. M said. "Your father told me he thought your birth certificate was with the rest of the papers he brought over with him, but he couldn't find it, just the baptism certificate. Which I've used plenty of times in the past."

Mr. Gibbs said that as far as he knew, nobody had ever questioned the authenticity of one of those baptism certificates until now. But that unfortunately, everything was different now in Little League baseball, especially in the Bronx, ever since Danny Almonte turned out to be older than he said he was.

"Gibbs said the bottom line was they had to take it to the District 22 board of directors," Mr. M said.

"And did they?" Michael said.

Mr. M said they'd just gotten off the conference call, and called Mr. Gibbs on his cell.

Michael could tell by the look on Mr. M's face that the news wasn't good.

"They decided that until a proper birth certificate is on file, you're not eligible to play," Mr. M said.

13

"I don't want you to worry about this," Mr. Minaya told Michael.

Yeah, right.

"Why are they doing this now?" Michael said.

"You know why."

"Because they don't believe I'm twelve," he said.

Mr. Minaya nodded. It was just the two of them sitting on the bench. The other kids were in a raggedy circle on the infield grass in front of home plate, eating the ice cream sandwiches Manny's mom had brought as the snack.

"Does the Grand Concourse coach think I'm not twelve?"

"No, he's on our side. He knows this is basically just sour grapes from Westchester South," Mr. Minaya said. "But he's one of the league commissioners and he's got to do his job. So when coaches file a complaint, he has to go by the rules, which we sort of bent when we accepted the baptism certificate."

"You said coaches," Michael said. "I thought it was just the coach of Westchester South."

Mr. Minaya put an arm around Michael. "He wrote the letter," he said. "But quite a few other coaches signed it."

"They all think I'm lying about my age?"

"No," Mr. Minaya said. "Just a bunch of coaches who think they're good enough to get to Williamsport this year, and that their chances improve tremendously if you're not pitching against them."

Now Michael didn't know what to say. It wasn't just Justin's dad. It was a whole gang of dads. Ganging up on him all of a sudden.

Mr. Minaya said, "This all got going because you showed up the man's son. I know it's probably going to be a pain in the butt for your father, because somehow he'll have to get help from somebody back in Cuba. He told me he probably could if he ever really had to." Mr. Minaya shrugged. "Well, now he really has to. You want to give me his number in Florida?"

Michael said, "No, it's okay. I'll tell him."

More than anything, Michael wanted to be eating ice cream with everybody else.

Be like everybody else.

"Mr. Gibbs said he's not even worried about it," Mr. Minaya said. "He joked with me that where he works during the day, he's got a lot more important things to sweat than pain-in-the-butt Little League parents."

Michael grabbed his bat and glove. "Where does Mr. Gibbs work?" he said.

"ACS," Mr. Minaya said. "Administration for Children's Services. It's a city agency, in charge of—"

Michael cut him off, not even worried that he might have sounded rude doing it.

"I know what they're in charge of," he said.

The next morning at breakfast Michael said to Carlos, "You're telling me there's nobody we can call back home to get me a birth certificate?"

"Papi used to say that if he ever asked somebody back in Havana for a favor like that, they would have thought he was *loco,*" Carlos said.

Crazy.

"But he had my baptism certificate instead?" Michael said. "You saw it?"

Carlos nodded. "Signed by Father Morales at San Antonia de

Padua. Papi held on to it like it was a ticket stub to heaven. And when he realized he didn't have the birth certificate, he went and got some kind of paper from Mr. Brown, way back at the start of the school year."

Mr. Brown was the principal at Michael's school, PS 31, the William Lloyd Garrison School on 156th Street.

Carlos said, "You'd think somebody would just stand up and tell this commissioner from the Pinstripers—"

"Mr. Gibbs," Michael said.

"—tell Mr. Gibbs that they're busting your chops for no good reason, and just make the whole thing go away," Carlos said. "I'd tell him myself, if he didn't turn out to be from the Administration for Children's Stinking Services."

"You'll figure something out," Michael said. "Just like you always do."

Carlos reached across the table, put out a closed fist for Michael to touch lightly with his own.

"My little *tipo,*" his big brother said.

Little man.

"If I was little," Michael said. "Or just more little than I am, maybe people wouldn't be saying I'm older than I am."

"That's a lie," Carlos said. "And we shouldn't have to prove a lie, Miguel."

"Carlos, how are we going to come up with a birth certificate if Papi couldn't?"

"When I figure that out," Carlos said, "you'll be the first to know."

After Carlos left for work, Michael went downstairs and used the key Mr. Ruiz had given him to the storage closet in the basement, got out his pitchback net, brought it outside, and set it up in the alley behind 825 Gerard.

He set the net up in its usual place, walked back to the little mound Mr. Ruiz had built up for him, with help from some friends of his from the Department of Public Works, who had been fixing potholes on 158th Street one day. Before the macadam had dried, Michael had run down to Stan's Sports World and bought a pitching rubber that he stuck on the top of it.

"Don't tell people I was the one," Mr. Ruiz said, giving Michael a wink. "I don't want them to think I'm a nice guy."

Michael had told him, "Your secret is safe with me." Then he grinned and added, "Besides, no one would believe me."

Now that pitcher's mound was his sanctuary. He threw easily at first, making sure to warm up the way he always did. Honoring his instrument, as Papi had always instructed him. Gradually, though, as he felt the familiar warmth in his arm—the heat—he began to throw harder and harder, even knowing that he required perfect control on the pitchback, that if he missed his spot and hit the net the wrong way the ball would go flying over his head and into the street.

Before long, it was as if Michael was trying to throw eighty on every single pitch, as if somehow he could strike them all out with fastballs, Justin the Jerk from Westchester South and his father and Mr. Gibbs of the ACS.

It's because they think I'm too good, Michael thought. And fired another one at the net, hitting it dead center.

I'm too good and they're acting like that's bad.

14

MICHAEL THOUGHT BY NOW HE WAS USED TO BEING ALONE, THAT IF THEY gave out awards for knowing how to be alone, he would win all of them.

He was more alone than ever now, without a baseball game to look forward to, not knowing if he would get to play again this year.

Because if there was a secret he had that felt almost as big as the one about Papi, it was this:

Baseball was Michael's real best friend. Even more than Manny.

Baseball was a constant companion for him, no matter how many times he came into the quiet of the empty apartment, especially at night. There was the game he had just played or the game he was getting ready to play, or the Yankee game, on the radio or on television.

There was no mother to make him a snack when he came through the door in the afternoon. There was no father now to sit with at the dinner table, the way he used to sit with Papi when he got home early enough, and talk about his day, or just talk about any silly old thing that came into his head. Most nights when he got back from a game, Carlos had left him food to heat up in the microwave Papi had bought for them a few weeks before he died.

Michael thought he knew everything about being alone, but somehow this was different.

He wasn't sad all the time, going through life with some kind of sad face on him. Papi always used to tell him and Carlos that anybody could get knocked down, it was how you picked yourself up that was important. How you got on with things. He had gotten on with things when he was the new boy in school, the one off the boat. He was proud of the way he had gotten on with things after they had lost Papi. And he knew there were plenty of things in his life to make him happy. Carlos could do it, when he would give Michael another pep talk about how it was the two of them against the world. Manny made him happy. Ellie made him happy, even though she seemed to be running away from him half the time.

Michael knew that if he ever tried to fumble around finding the right words—as good as he had gotten with his English in the last year—and tried to explain what he was feeling right now to Manny, how alone he really felt, his friend would give him one of his wall-to-wall smiles and say, "But, Star, how can you be alone when you've got me?"

Even Manny wasn't enough, not right now.

Baseball made Michael feel normal. It made him feel as if he had turned back the clock, that things were the way they used to be, before Papi died. Before Carlos became the man of the house, before they both had to live in fear of all these Official Persons, whether they worked for the Bronx borough president or the Administration for Children's Services.

Before.

It was why Michael never complained along with the rest of the Clippers when one of their games ran long. A pitcher would start walking the whole world and the game would go past two hours, and everybody would act like they couldn't get off the field soon enough.

Michael never cared how long the games took.

Because when the game ended, he knew the next stop for him was the empty apartment at 825 Gerard.

Manny called him "Star" and Michael let him, because Michael treated it like a joke, one more joke between the two of them, part of why they were the kind of friends they were. So Manny got to call him something that Michael would never ever call himself.

But with all that, Michael knew how good he was at baseball. He didn't need Manny to tell him, he hadn't even needed Papi to tell him. He knew what he could do when he had a ball in his hand.

Now that ball had been taken away from him.

It turned out the only team in the league that could beat him was a team of coaches.

He talked himself into going to the next Clippers game, the last game of the regular season, the one that could clinch first place for them, telling himself that being around the team would make him feel a little better. A little less alone, just for one night.

It made him feel worse.

The game was at Castle Hill, against the Castle Hill Hilltoppers. Michael had originally been scheduled to pitch four innings, maybe more if his pitch count was as low as it usually was. Not only was first place on the line, and the top seed in the District 22 play-offs, but there was more than a week before the play-offs started, so Michael would have had plenty of time off.

He had gone back and forth all day about going to the game. Finally, about five o'clock, Manny had talked him into it. "You get to spend the night with me, or being a mope," Manny said. "I think your choice is clear." So Michael had put on his uniform and taken the ride in the old blue bus over to Castle Hill, sitting in the same backseat he always did, next to Manny.

"I'm going to show everybody I'm a team guy, even when I'm not on the team," he said to Manny.

"Right," Manny said. "It's been keeping me up nights, worrying whether you were a team guy or not."

"You know what I'm saying."

"Actually, I do."

Michael brought two gloves with him, his regular one and the left-handed catcher's mitt Papi had found for him in a sporting goods store up near Fordham Road, just in case Manny ever missed a game. When the starting players were out on the field for infield practice, Michael warmed up Anthony Fierro, who was starting in his place.

He told Mr. M he would coach first base once the game started, and did, taking the job seriously, watching for all of Mr. M's complicated signs, making sure the base runner was paying attention in case Mr. M was calling for a steal.

When he was on the bench, he was full of chatter, encouraging whoever was at the plate, trying to be the best baseball cheerleader in the Bronx on this night. Michael tried to smile through it all. Even though he felt like he was on the outside of everything, despite how close he was to the action, the way he always felt like he was on the outside of Yankee Stadium. Even with it standing right there in front of him, bigger than life.

The Clippers won, 5–4. Anthony pitched the best he had all year, even cleared the fence with a three-run homer. He went four innings and Kel, with all his slow stuff, this little dinky pitch he had that always seemed to find the outside corner, pitched the last two.

But the play of the game came from Maria, a game-saver with two outs in the bottom of the last inning, runners on second and third. There was a slow roller to her at second, a ball past the pitcher's mound that Kel just barely missed. Maria had stopped for a moment, thinking Kel was going to get it. Then she came hard. Too late, Michael thought from where he was standing in front of the Clippers' bench. The Hilltoppers were going to tie the game at least, and have the winning run on third.

But Maria Cuellar wasn't thinking that way. She was about to make the play of her life, barehanding the ball the way a big-league third baseman does with a bunt, dipping her body to the right, underhanding it in almost the same motion to Anthony, who was finishing the game at first base.

It all seemed to happen at once then, Maria falling to the infield grass, Anthony stretching for the throw, the umpire hustling up the line from home plate to throw up his arm and call "Out!" as Maria's throw got the Hilltopper batter by a step.

Even without Michael on the mound, the Clippers had still managed to hold on to first place. Now, for the first time all night, he felt like he was a part of things, felt happy for his teammates, beating everybody on the bench out to the crowd of Clippers jumping up and down near first base.

After Michael had congratulated Kel for closing the deal, he saw Manny standing on the mound, cap backward on his head, mask in one hand and mitt in the other.

"That was the greatest ending of the whole year!" he shouted at Michael.

Michael came over to him, grinning. "Only because it gave you a chance to hug Maria."

"Shut up," Manny said. Then the two of them gave each other five, first up high, then down low.

As they walked off the field, Manny said, "You sure you're all right?"

"We won," Michael said. "I don't know what it would've been like if we lost. But we didn't lose. I told you all year this team would be good enough to make it to Williamsport without me."

Manny put an arm around Michael's shoulder. "Star?"

"What?"

"Let's not get carried away."

"I'm cool," Michael said.

Just less cool, a lot less, when he looked up and saw the Grand Concourse coach, the man from the ACS, standing behind their bench, motioning to Michael that he wanted to talk to him.

"Remember me?" he asked, sticking out a hand that Michael thought was surprisingly small for a man. "My name's Tony Gibbs."

Michael shook it. "I know who you are," he said. "From the other night."

"I'm happy things worked out all right for you guys," Mr. Gibbs said. "But I'm sorry you couldn't play."

"Me, too," Michael said.

"Rules are rules," Mr. Gibbs said, "even when they're dumb rules that grown-ups came up with."

"Yeah."

"I left a message at your apartment," Mr. Gibbs said. "Then I tried the work number your father left on file. At the car service."

Michael couldn't catch his breath. Felt like he did one time when he wasn't looking and a hard throw from Anthony had hit him in the stomach. . . .

"They said he hadn't been there for a few months," Mr. Gibbs said.

Michael thought to himself: Is that all it's been? But he knew Mr. Gibbs was right. Papi had died in May. Now it was August.

It just seemed so much farther away sometimes.

Something that happened in the life he and Carlos and Papi used to have. Now Michael wanted Carlos here with him. Right here, right now, telling him the right things to say.

The right lies to tell.

"My uncle . . . ," he started to say.

"Yeah, I know, he's sick in Florida, that's why your dad has been away."

"But he'll be back soon," Michael said. "My father. Really."

Really?

Where the heck did that come from?

"How're you guys getting by, him being away this long?" Mr. Gibbs said.

"My brother has two jobs!" Michael said.

Too loud, too fast.

"Good for him," Mr. Gibbs said, smiling at Michael, as if neither one of them had a thing to worry about, he was just asking a few questions here, like a teacher going over a simple homework assignment.

Like they were on the same page.

Even though Michael knew they weren't even in the same book.

"Has he come back and forth at all?"

"Who?"

"Your dad. From Florida."

"One time," Michael said. "He drove all the way back a few weeks ago, when he thought my uncle was starting to get better."

A good lie, Michael decided. Good boy. Not too big a lie, that was the key. Carlos had been saying all along that the simpler the lie, the easier it was to remember.

Mr. Gibbs wore a gray Special Olympics sweatshirt and blue jeans and old running shoes and a black baseball cap that said Arthur Ashe Foundation over the bill. Behind him Michael could see his teammates packing up their gear, the ones who needed a ride getting ready to board the bus for the drive back across the Bronx to Macombs Dam Park, where they'd get picked up by the parents who hadn't made the game.

Mr. Gibbs sat down on the bench and patted the spot next to him, as if he and Michael had all night. When he took off his cap, Michael saw a lot of curly black hair.

He was young for an Official Person, Michael thought. He'd always thought of them as being older than churches.

"Well, you probably know why I'm here, kiddo. We gotta come up with that birth certificate, and fast."

"My brother has been trying to call some of my father's old friends in Havana," Michael said. "And my father, of course he's been doing the same from my uncle's."

"Understand, we told the coaches who made the complaint that we're comfortable with what we already have. But they've called the folks at the District Office. And the District Office says that because you're such a great pitcher, and because your team has such a great chance to make it to the World Series, they don't want there to be any controversy, the way there was a few years ago."

"When Danny Almonte lied about his age," Michael said.

"You know about him?"

"Everybody in the Bronx does."

Michael imagined a tennis ball bouncing back and forth across a net.

"I want to help," Mr. Gibbs said.

Michael wanted to say, Sure you do.

"Thank you," is what he did say.

"Tell you what," Mr. Gibbs said. "If your dad's not back next week, why don't I stop by the apartment and see if I can help your brother out? This is a pretty complicated job for a seventeen-year-old kid."

"Okay," Michael said.

"I know this probably doesn't make any sense to you," Mr. Gibbs said. "Sometimes it's the grown-ups who act like children."

Michael heard Mr. Minaya yelling at everybody that he could still see a lot of garbage, to get back there and police the area one last time.

"For what it's worth, Michael," Mr. Gibbs said, "I'm on your side. I work with a lot of kids around your age, and I think I know a fourteen-year-old when I see one. Or at least like to think I do."

"I'm twelve," Michael said.

Then he couldn't help it, this wasn't one of the times he could stop himself, he started to cry.

"Hey," Mr. Gibbs said, putting an arm around him. "Everything's going to be fine."

Michael nodded as if agreeing with him, rubbing his eyes as he did, feeling like the dope of all times, the dope of the whole stupid world, hoping that nobody on his team could see him acting like a baby.

"I know," Michael said.

"You know what they say, right?" Mr. Gibbs said, still wanting to be his friend.

Somehow Michael knew what was coming next.

"No crying in baseball," Mr. Gibbs said. "Not even Little League baseball."

Manny tried to pump Michael for information on the ride home. Michael told him they could talk about it on the phone later, he didn't want anybody else on the bus to hear.

"You're asking me to be patient?" Manny said. "You know I don't do patient."

"Just this once."

"Okay," Manny said. "But let's not make a habit of it."

Mr. M did what he'd been doing the whole All-Star season when the Clippers had an away game, dropping Michael in front of 825 Gerard and not pulling away with the old bus until Michael was inside the front door. Everybody on the team knew that Carlos worked most nights and had heard the story about the sick uncle in

Florida and thought Victor Arroyo was still away. So nobody thought this was star treatment for Michael.

Even if they did, Manny always pointed out, nobody would have given a rat's rear end. His words.

Michael told Manny to call when he got home, promising he'd tell him everything about his conversation with Mr. Gibbs. Then he got out of the bus, ran up the front steps, took the stairs up to the apartment, unlocked the door, made himself a humongous chocolate milk shake, remembered with a slap to his forehead that the Yankees were on Channel 9 tonight. Regular TV.

He could watch.

They were playing the Texas Rangers at home. The announcers were saying that tonight had been Family Night at the Stadium, and there had been a one-inning game before the start of the regular one that involved some of the Yankees and their children, that was why the Yankees-Rangers game had been a little late in starting.

Keith Wright, the Yankees' rookie left-hander, was pitching tonight, and had a 2–0 lead in the third inning.

Michael sat on the couch, happy as always to have the Yankees as company in the empty apartment.

On the screen, Keith Wright threw a big, slow, breaking curveball that seemed to come up to the plate as slowly as the one that El Grande liked to throw. When the batter missed it by a mile, the camera went into the Yankee dugout, and found El Grande sitting there with a couple of teammates, pointing at Keith Wright and laughing his head off.

Then the camera went to a box near the Yankee dugout, where Michael Kay, the Yankees' play-by-play man, said El Grande's family was sitting tonight. Saying that it was unusual for the children to be here, they usually only came when their father was the one throwing the big, slow, breaking curveballs.

A little girl's face filled the screen. Michael Kay said that was El Grande's three-year-old daughter, Adriana. While the camera was on her, she turned and tried to climb over her seat into the box behind her, her mother grabbing her from behind right before she went up and over.

"The older daughter," Michael Kay continued, "is named Elisa."

"That's right, Michael," Jim Kaat, the Yankees' other broadcaster, said. "Elisa Garcia Gonzalez. A name as pretty as she is."

Michael stared at the screen.

"She's beautiful," Michael Kay said.

"No," Michael Arroyo said. "She's Ellie."

15

THE OFFICE OF THE BRONX BOROUGH PRESIDENT, MR. AMOROSA, WAS LOcated on the Grand Concourse. And for all the worrying Michael had done about going there and having his picture taken with Mr. Amorosa and Officer Crandall and Mrs. C, the whole thing had been about as exciting as posing for some dopey class picture.

Carlos went along, too, getting the morning off from the Imperial, switching shifts with a friend. When Mr. Amorosa asked about their dad, Mrs. C stepped right up and said she was standing in for him, once again being their honorary grandma, and that her dear, dear friend Victor Arroyo sent his deepest regrets from his brother's bedside in Florida.

When Mr. Amorosa said he'd say a prayer for the uncle, Mrs. C made the sign of the cross.

Knowing Mrs. C's theories about sin, Michael figured she'd be on her way to confession as soon as they were done.

There were four photographers in front of Mr. Amorosa's building. Michael wore his white church-shirt with the stiff collar and the tie Carlos had given him, one that was way too long for him. When they were in place on the front steps, Mr. Amorosa stepped to the microphone that had been set up there, even though there was no crowd to watch them, just the photographers. He presented Michael with a baseball signed by the Yankee starting pitchers, including El Grande, and a Bronx Good Citizen plaque with Michael's name on it, and a brief description of how he had "felled"—that was the word they used—a robbery with courage and quick thinking.

Then Mr. Amorosa made a brief speech in which he said pretty much the same things that were written on the plaque.

"We hear all the time in baseball about pitchers mowing batters down," Mr. Amorosa said. "This time a fine young man from our borough mowed down a petty criminal who had preyed on this sweet old woman standing next to me."

The ceremony took ten minutes, tops. When they were done, Mr. Amorosa posed one more time, shaking Michael's hand as the photographers took their pictures. Then he wished him luck in the upcoming play-offs, even saying he might try to catch a game. Michael knew there was probably as much chance of that as Mr. Amorosa wading into the Harlem River and catching fish with his bare hands.

When they were finished, Michael noticed that the cameras disappeared almost as quickly as Mr. Amorosa did. Carlos asked Michael if he wanted to ride back home in the car Mr. Amorosa's office had provided. Michael said, no, he and Manny would walk.

Michael had asked Manny to tag along, knowing he would. This was a big event in Manny's eyes, even if it didn't include him. He lived for events of any kind. Big games. School field trips, even if they involved going to art museums. School plays. The opening of any new movie they really wanted to see, even if it meant getting permission to take the subway all the way to Times Square and pay their way into one of the massive theaters Manny called plexi-plexes.

As soon as they were back on the street in front of 851 Grand Concourse, Michael yanked off his tie as if it had been a noose around his neck, and stuffed it into the pocket of his Old Navy khakis.

"What did I tell you?" Manny said. "No problemo."

"Yeah, we had him all the way," Michael said. "I wish I could get Mr. ACS Man off my back that easy."

"We'll think of something," Manny said.

"You just keep thinking, Butch," Michael said to Manny, using one of his favorite lines from *Butch Cassidy and the Sundance Kid,* one of his favorite movies. "That's what you're good at."

"You should have gone along with my brilliant idea about a fake dad," Manny said.

"Why," Michael said, "so the fake dad can come up with a fake birth certificate?"

"You know what I'm saying."

"Not always," Michael said, poking Manny with an elbow.

They were in no hurry to get back to Gerard Avenue. No hurry to do anything, really. The sound of the day, of the city, was all around them, as loud and busy as ever. It was another reason, Michael thought, why he loved baseball so much, loved the idea that all the action didn't start until he started it by going into his motion. There he'd be, alone on the mound, the ball in his hand, the ball feeling as small sometimes in his palm as a marble, almost like he was alone in his own world, not even hearing the infield chatter from behind him.

Sometimes Michael thought the two most quiet places in his whole world were the pitcher's mound and the apartment at night before he put the Yankee game on.

Manny said, "Well, are we gonna talk about her ever?"

He poked Michael now, as if waking him up.

"How much more can we talk about her?" Michael said. "She's not just a girl. She's El Grande's daughter. That happens to mean she's living in a whole different world than we're living in."

"But she's been hanging around in our world 'cause she wants to," Manny said. "Nobody made her."

"Why couldn't she just have told us who she really was?"

"Because," Manny said, "she was probably afraid you'd get your panties in a wad exactly the way they are right now." He put both hands over his heart, put his head back, closed his eyes. "Oh," he said, "I am just a poor Cuban boy from the wrong side of the subway tracks, and am not worthy. . . ."

That was as far as he got before Michael stepped back and gave him a soccer-style kick to the seat of his pants.

"Hey!" Manny said. "That actually hurt."

"Good."

"She likes you," Manny said now.

"It doesn't change who she is."

"I know," Manny said. "She's the great man's daughter. And yet she keeps coming around."

"At least now we know why she only showed up on days he was pitching," Michael said. "She must come in with him instead of her mom, and then get a little bored just hanging around the ballpark."

"I told you: She likes you," Manny said. "Deal with it."

"She doesn't like me enough to tell me the truth."

"Hey, jerkwad," Manny said. "Maybe you've noticed, people sometimes have a good reason for holding stuff back."

As usual when it turned into a debate, Manny had him.

They had walked long enough now that the Stadium was in front of them.

Manny told Michael to hang on, ran into a convenience store, came out with a couple of Snapple iced teas, with lemon, and handed one to Michael.

"Where do you suppose she lives?" Manny said.

"Riverdale," Michael said.

"You know that?"

"I read it in the papers."

Riverdale, they both knew, was the most expensive part of the Bronx, like a whole different Bronx, up off the Henry Hudson

Parkway, with big old brick mansions looking like castles guarding the river below. Michael had seen those mansions once on a boat trip up the Hudson their sixth-grade class had taken.

"She could have told me," Michael said one more time, being stubborn the way he was with pitches sometimes, going for a particular corner of the plate, inside or outside, even when he was missing.

"Are you thick or what?" Manny said. "She probably only hangs around with kids who can't get over the fact that she's El Grande's daughter, look at her for herself. And then she finds us and it's completely different, we don't know anything, we just like her for her. You and your faithful companion."

"Which would be you."

"Friends to the end," Manny said. "And then five days after that."

They touched their Snapple bottles together.

"I want to see her again," Michael said. Even though the thought now scared him.

"Duh," Manny said.

"You think she'll come around when the Yankees are home next week?"

"Duh," Manny said again.

"But what if she thinks I saw her on TV and now I know who she is and she just doesn't want me to turn into another El Grande groupie?"

"Star?"

"What?"

"Will you listen to me for one second?"

"All I do is listen to you."

"I mean really listen," Manny said. "You've got enough crummy stuff going on in your life. They won't even let you play right now.

But Ellie isn't part of that. Ellie is a good thing. A good problem to have. Am I right?"

Michael mumbled his reply, on purpose.

"I didn't quite catch that," Manny said.

"I said, you're right."

Manny Cabrera, light on his feet as always, more graceful than all the people who called him No Neck knew, danced now on the Bronx street corner, Michael's catcher celebrating as if he'd just scored a touchdown.

16

Tony Gibbs had spent most of the morning at a group home just up the block from the basketball courts at Rosedale Park. It had been a good morning. No, a great morning, because of the news Gibbs had delivered there to a twelve-year-old orphan named Beliz Ortega.

Both of Beliz Ortega's parents had been killed on 9/11, the father a security man in the North Tower and the mother a receptionist at a bond-trading company on the 101st floor, the two of them thrilled because they could make the long train ride to work together every morning. Beliz was an only child. He had gone into the foster-care system and ended up at this group home.

Now Tony Gibbs told the boy that he had a foster home for him in Ridgewood, New Jersey.

Gibbs lived for these days.

Beliz Ortega had met the foster parents twice, first when they came to visit him in the group home, the second time an overnight visit, approved by the ACS, to the family's home in Ridgewood. After that, as always, came the worst part for these kids, the waiting period to find out whether or not they had made the cut. Sometimes this went on for weeks, before some family decided they didn't want some twelve-year-old Dominican or fourteen-year-old Puerto Rican. Then Gibbs had to sit them down and tell them they hadn't gotten into the only club that any of them cared about.

A real home.

But this time they said yes. The Kimballs were an older couple with kids already through college. They had decided they wanted children in the house again, had talked about various modern-day options. China. Romania. Then it turned out they had a friend who had joined the board of New Yorkers for Children, the city's best foster-care charity. The friend had put them in touch with one of Gibbs's bosses at ACS. Finally there came the day when the Kimballs came across the George Washington Bridge to say yes.

Days like this didn't wipe out a hundred bad days for Tony Gibbs, just carried him to the next good one. So on this morning he helped Beliz Ortega, a kid with the face of an angel, to pack his cheap bag, then walked him out the front door with the Kimballs, all of them turning around when they heard the cheers from the other kids in the group home hanging out the window.

Gibbs cheered along with them.

He hugged the boy and told him to have a great life and watched the Kimballs' Toyota SUV with Jersey plates pull away.

He thought about going back to his office then, in the Bronx borough president's office on the Grand Concourse. Instead, because he hadn't gotten a chance to make his morning run along the East River today, he decided to make the long walk across the Bronx to Yankee Stadium, where he knew the Yankees were playing an afternoon game. He knew one of the cops who worked security outside the Stadium. When Gibbs would show up after the game had started, whether it was a sellout or not, the guy would wave him in and tell him to go find an empty seat.

Gibbs loved the Yankees almost as much as he loved helping these stray kids.

Now he walked for an hour, forgetting how far it was from Rosedale Park to the Stadium, hailed a cab, got out on 161st Street.

161st and Gerard.

It made him think of Michael Arroyo, just because the kid had been on his mind a lot lately.

Gibbs didn't walk up 161st toward the Stadium. He hung a left and started walking up Gerard instead, pulling out his wallet as he did, making sure he had the address right.

He had done this sort of work a long time, working even harder at it after his divorce, throwing himself into the job with a vengeance. By now he had a sixth sense about kids, whether they were in the system or not, whether they were on his Bronx Little League team or not.

Something wasn't right in Michael Arroyo's life, he was sure of it.

Tony Gibbs had a feeling, one of his famous gut instincts, that the kid's old man had run out on them.

He saw the boy before he got to the entrance to 825 Gerard, in an alley behind the building, throwing to one of those old-fashioned pitchbacks. Gibbs stood across the street, watched that beautiful motion he saw from the boy in games, the high kick, that perfect arm angle of his, the ball coming straight over the top.

Like Koufax, his all-time hero.

Not many people remembered Sandy Koufax anymore. Maybe it was because Gibbs's dad had been an old Brooklyn Dodger fan, one of the few who still rooted for them after they left for Los Angeles. They would watch Koufax when Tony was little and his father would always remind him that Koufax had started in Brooklyn as a kid.

Now he watched this Little League boy who he believed had some Koufax in him, the boy lost in what he was doing, taking it seriously, then throwing another one with all his might that hit the net in a place that sent the ball right back to him like it was on a string.

Gibbs thought: This is better than anything I'm going to watch today with the Yankees and Devil Rays.

This kid is the real deal.

A car horn finally distracted Michael Arroyo and he threw one too high, and the ball came flying back over his head, right through the entrance to the small alley and across the street to where Gibbs was standing.

When Michael turned around, there he was.

"Michael, I'd like to ask you a question," Tony Gibbs said, picking up the ball, tossing it back with a little zip on it. "Where's your father, really?"

For some reason, Michael tossed the ball back to the ACS man, who caught it easily with his right hand. Just doing that, feeling the baseball in his hand, then throwing it to him, made Michael feel better, as if he could somehow pitch his way out of this jam.

"What do you mean?" Michael said.

"No games, Michael. Where's your father?"

The two of them kept playing catch, Mr. Gibbs on his side of 158th Street, Michael at the entrance to the alley. Mr. Gibbs was wearing blue jeans again, a different sweatshirt this time, one that said New Yorkers for Children.

Michael wondered if he was one of those children.

"My father's in Florida," Michael said.

"Tell me the town again?" Mr. Gibbs said.

He made it sound casual. Like they'd had this conversation before. But Michael knew they had never talked about what town Victor Arroyo was supposed to be in, visiting the sick brother who did not exist. Michael knew and Mr. Gibbs knew. He remembered watching *Law & Order* one time with Carlos and Carlos saying,

"Lawyers never ask questions they don't already know the answers to."

What did Mr. Gibbs of the ACS really know, now that he'd come around asking where Michael's father really was?

"It's near Miami," Michael said. "Carlos knows. The only thing I know about Miami is that the Marlins play there, and beat the Yankees that time in the Series."

"When did he go down there?" Mr. Gibbs said. He didn't want to talk about the Yankees and Marlins. "I mean, exactly?" he said.

He came over now to where Michael was, sat down inside the alley, his back against the wire fence. Michael noticed his sneakers. He always noticed sneakers, maybe because his were always so worn-down, having to last him from the start of one school year to the start of the next. Mr. Gibbs's soft old Reeboks looked like they were almost as old as Mrs. C.

"It was right around when I got out of school," Michael said. "Or a little before, maybe."

Keep the lies simple.

"Yeah, that's what they said at that car service," Mr. Gibbs said. "But your dad only works there part-time, right?"

"He owns his car," Michael said. "He likes to be on his own, my father. But they would call him when they needed extra drivers."

"They said the eighteenth of May was the last time they heard from him," Mr. Gibbs said.

"Yes," Michael said.

Yes. He said it very clearly. Papi never allowed yeah. Speak American, he always said. You're American now. Yes, Michael was thinking, May 18 was the last time the car service had heard from his father because that was the day his father had died.

"So he's been gone awhile now," Mr. Gibbs said. "He must really trust you and your brother."

"Carlos says he's like the dad who had to come off the bench," Michael said.

"You're sure he didn't just take off?" Mr. Gibbs said. "Your father, I mean. It's a terrible thing to say, I know, but I see it in my job all the time."

"He's with my uncle," Michael said. "Why don't you believe me?"

He wanted Manny to come walking right around that corner now, Michael knowing that all he had to do was give Manny a look and his friend would know he needed help, as though Michael had sent an instant-message right into his brain.

Or he wanted Mrs. C to come walking up the hill from the Imperial.

Or Carlos.

Anybody.

"Hey, relax," Mr. Gibbs said. "It's my job to ask questions like this."

"To everybody?"

"When I think there's a problem."

"My uncle's the problem, is all," Michael said.

"What's his name, your uncle?"

Shoot.

"Luis," Michael said.

There had been an old Yankee pitcher he knew about, just because they had the same last name. Luis Arroyo. He had first read about him in a book about Yogi Berra he had taken out of the library.

Mr. Gibbs said, "Hey, that's funny, there was a relief pitcher once, had that same name, Luis Arroyo. But that was before your time."

"My father told me about him," Michael lied.

"Did Uncle Luis come over on the boat with you?"

"No, he came a few years before."

Lie after lie after lie.

"And he doesn't have family of his own, down there in Miami, to take care of him?"

Michael said, "They stayed behind when he left, and then they didn't want to come later."

The questions were coming faster now. Michael felt the way he did when he sat in the subway car and the train was outside, and everything was flying past him.

No one said anything now, for what felt like a long time, until Mr. Gibbs said, "There's no uncle, is there, Michael?"

Michael took the ball out of his glove, bounced it off the pavement as if it were a basketball, did that hard once, then twice.

"You're calling me a liar?" he said.

"I think the lie is that your dad is ever coming back."

"No!" Michael shouted. "You've got it all wrong, you'll see."

"Will I?" Mr. Gibbs said. "My line of work, Michael? My job? I see parents running out all the time, for a million different reasons. It's not your fault, or your brother's, if he did."

Michael didn't know what to say to that.

"I can help you," Mr. Gibbs said. "You don't have to be afraid of me."

He looked up at him, tipped an old Yankees cap back on his head.

"I'm one of the good guys," he said.

Michael blinked fast and hard a few times, determined not to start crying, because this was another time when he knew crying would be like some kind of confession on *Law & Order.*

"If he's gone, you gotta tell me."

Gone, Michael thought to himself. Like Papi had gone out for cigars and never come back.

"My brother and I are fine," Michael said. "We don't need your help."

"The two of you are too young to be living alone for this long."

"That's the thing," Michael said. "We aren't going to be living alone much longer."

The words were out of his mouth before Michael could stop them, like a cartoon genie blowing out of the bottle.

"So your father's finally coming home?" Mr. Gibbs said.

"Day after tomorrow," Michael said.

17

MICHAEL WATCHED AS MANNY ACTUALLY BEGAN TO TALK CARLOS INTO IT. It being his big idea that his uncle Timo, who had gotten some small parts in off-Broadway plays and even in some of the television shows shot in New York, could play the part of Papi, just for one day.

They were in the living room. Michael had called Manny as soon as Mr. Gibbs had left, told Manny what he had told Mr. Gibbs about his father coming back the day after tomorrow. He had also told Manny to get his butt over to 825 Gerard before Carlos got home from the Imperial.

"Why do you need me?" Manny said.

"As moral support," Michael said.

"As a human shield," Manny said, and then told Michael he'd be right over.

Michael expected Carlos to yell when he told him about Mr. Gibbs. But he didn't yell, or walk out of the room. He just sat there on the couch, still in his Imperial white shirt and tie, and listened to Manny, as if Manny were now the one in charge here.

"This can work," Manny said.

"I told you," Carlos said, "I'm listening."

"We can make sure Uncle Timo's English is a lot worse than your father's really was," Manny said, "that way he can act confused if he has to. Then all he has to do is keep thanking Mr. Gibbs for being this interested in his boys, tell him he's working day and night to get that stinking birth certificate, and that hopefully he'll see us all at the Little League World Series."

Manny stood up, bowed at the waist, then said, "You've been a great audience, don't forget to tip your waiters."

Michael had no idea what that one meant. He just laughed along with Carlos, who did seem to understand. Michael did this a lot, laughed at something Manny said even if Manny seemed to be saying it in some kind of foreign language.

Carlos said, "You're good, Manuel. And I'm sure your uncle is. But what if he makes a slip?"

"Let me ask you a question," Manny said. "What have we got to lose? This Mr. Gibbs was sure your father had just deserted you guys. Which means he's going to keep coming around like the truant officer unless we do something."

"I'm not saying we're just going to sit around and do nothing," Carlos said. "I'm just asking what happens if I agree to go along with your crazy plan and Uncle Timo makes a slip."

"He won't."

"How do you know that?"

"Because I know my uncle," Manny said. "My mother says he could sell sand in the desert."

"He would do this? Your uncle?"

"He's my godfather," Manny said. "He knows I look up to him, even though he's not close to being a star, because I think maybe I'd like to be an actor someday. If I ask him, yeah, I think he'll do it."

Carlos went into the kitchen, came back with a Coke, and sat down now in Papi's old recliner, with the tape on one of the arms and the cushion.

"This is crazy," Carlos said.

"Our whole life is crazy," Michael said.

"I'm telling you, this'll work," Manny said. "You and Michael can tell him everything he needs to know, and he can memorize it!" Michael saw that look come over his friend's face again. His big-idea look. "We can even have one of those mock debates like we do in class before a real debate. And you can pretend you're Mr. Gibbs and fire questions at him."

Carlos looked at Michael, then Manny, then back to Michael.

"I can't believe I'm letting you two knotheads talk me into this," he said. "Working two jobs must be making me way too tired."

"I promise, this is gonna be great!" Manny said.

Michael thought: Manny Cabrera is the one who could sell sand in the desert.

"We just need to give him something so he stops coming around, until you figure out a way to get that stupid birth certificate, Carlos."

"I called Father Morales," Carlos said. "Our old pastor. He was on vacation, but the priest who answered said he'd give him the message as soon as he got back."

"So for now, we work on Uncle Timo," Manny said, clapping his hands. "We gotta keep you guys together."

Carlos smiled and said to Michael, *"Al pan pan y al vino vino."*

"Hey," Manny said, "no keeping secrets."

"You never heard that one?" Carlos said.

"All I got was the wine part," Manny said.

Michael said, "It's a Cuban expression, about bread and wine. But it's really about calling things as they are, no lies."

"Until the next lie," Carlos said.

"You guys call bread and wine whatever you want," Manny said. "I'm gonna call Uncle Timo."

"You're actually going to let us do this?" Michael said to Carlos before his brother went off to work at Hector's. As always, his brother was wearing his favorite baseball cap, the one with the *W* on the front, which Michael knew was for the old Washington Senators, even if the new Nationals team was using a *W* on its caps now.

Papi had loved the Senators when he was a boy, even though they were usually terrible, because their star pitcher was Camilo Pascual, a Cuban by birth.

"I am *thinking* about letting you do this," Carlos said, checking himself out in the mirror, making sure the cap was just so. "Just because a few minutes with this Uncle Timo guy might get Mr. Gibbs off our backs."

He pointed a finger at Michael, then Manny, then back at Michael. "But remember, you two, nothing happens with Uncle Timo until I get to meet him tomorrow."

Michael said, "I'm just going to tell him stuff about Papi's life. Tell him some baseball things about the two of us. And Manny thinks we should show him some pictures of all of us."

"And don't forget to show him some of the Cuban expressions I wrote up," Carlos said.

"Do you think Mr. Gibbs will know the difference?" Manny said.

"Aquí hay gato encerrado," Carlos said to Manny.

"Say what?"

"He's saying there's a caged cat here," Michael said. "And the cat is me."

"I just want to make sure the cat has nine lives," Carlos said.

It got a smile out of Michael, not easy these days. "How many lives do I have left?" he said to his brother.

"That's what we're trying to find out, Miguel," his brother said, and left for work.

Uncle Timo showed up about an hour later, wearing a short-sleeved shirt outside his jeans, sandals, no socks. He was still wearing his sunglasses, even though the sun was gone from the sky, and wearing the kind of backpack Michael and Manny took to school with them.

He looked old enough to be a dad to teenaged boys, Michael thought. He even had a beard that reminded Michael a little bit of the neat, trimmed beard Papi always had.

Uncle Timo was carrying a plastic bottle of water.

"Dude!" he said to Manny when he came through the door, giving Manny a big hug. "Now you think you've turned into my agent?"

Michael's heart fell now, hard, as if he'd dropped it from a high place.

Uncle Timo sounded more American than baseball announcers.

"And you," he said, rubbing Michael's head, "must be the famous Mike." He stepped back and put out his hand. "Gimme some," he said.

Michael gave him five, but without too much enthusiasm. Uncle Timo noticed it, because he dropped his head to the side and gave Michael a funny look. "Where's the love, dude?"

"Don't worry," Manny said, reading Michael's mind, as usual. "He grows on you."

Uncle Timo dropped his backpack on the floor and plopped himself down in Papi's old recliner chair. "My nephew here gave me the setup," he said. "And, by the way, dude, I'm sorry about your pop."

"Thank you," Michael said.

Thinking to himself: He's more of a teenager than Carlos is!

"Manny laid out the plot for me," Uncle Timo said. "I'm Dad, I've been down in Florida, I'm back for a day, just to check in on my boys, then I'm back down there with my illin' brother."

"Illin'?" Michael said.

"Sick," Manny said, then grinned and said, "dude."

"What if Mr. Gibbs asks where your brother is?"

"Got it covered," Uncle Timo said. "I got a girl down there, her own place in Homestead. Working a dinner theater down there. He calls that number, she's the maid, not so good *habla*ing the *Inglesia*."

Michael closed his eyes.

"Besides," Uncle Timo said, "Manny said all we've got to do is convince The Man"—he made little quotation marks with his fingers around the last two words—"that I'm the man of the house, and that I trust you guys to keep things under control till I get back."

Manny said, "Sounds like a plan."

"Manny says the guy thinks your dad turned deadbeat and ran out on you?"

Michael looked at Manny. "He knows the whole story," Manny said.

"You can't tell," Michael said to Uncle Timo.

"Dude," Uncle Timo said, sounding hurt.

Michael noticed that every time Uncle Timo said "dude," he sounded more like Manny. Or Kel.

Even more like a kid.

"Seriously," he said to Michael, "don't worry, I don't spill my guts unless I'm getting paid to do it on a cop show."

Michael said, "The one you have to fool? Mr. Gibbs? He's very smart. So you've got to be good."

"I am good," he said. "My agent tells me all the time."

Michael wasn't so sure. Uncle Timo was a goof. But at least he was trying.

"What do you want to know about my father?" Michael said.

"First I want to see him," Uncle Timo said. "Manny said you've got pictures."

"But I don't understand why you need them," Michael said.

"Because if I'm going to be him, I need to know what he looks like."

"But you don't look anything like him, except for maybe your beard."

"I don't look like him yet," Uncle Timo said.

"Yet?"

"That happens," he said, "when the magic happens, kid."

Michael went into his room, reached up to the shelf in his closet, got down the shoe box with some of Papi's stuff in it: the small stack of photographs that the nice woman, a stranger, had offered to take at the Bronx Zoo that time; Papi's cigar cutter; the old black-and-white team photograph of the Cuban National Team, with Papi standing next to a smiling, happy batboy at the end, one who didn't look much older than Michael was now. Papi said the boy had snuck into the clubhouse that morning, just wanting to see some of his heroes. The manager of the team wanted to throw him out. But Papi had liked the spunk it had taken to sneak in there. Then he had proclaimed the kid batboy for a day, he told Michael every time he retold the story, and had gotten him into the team picture.

There was the photo of Michael and Papi posing outside Yankee Stadium, next to the huge bat that rose like a skyscraper.

There was the picture of Papi standing proudly next to his Grand Prix. Finally there was the photograph that was Michael's favorite, from the spring, not so long before Papi had his heart attack:

Michael in his Modell Monuments uniform, Papi with his arm around him, both of them smiling. Michael remembered Papi telling him that day that now he really was an official American boy. He was in Little League.

Only now he wasn't in Little League. . . .

Michael brought the box into the living room, set it on the glass coffee table, took out the Little League picture and showed that one to Uncle Timo first. He carefully took the photograph out of Michael's hand, stared at it hard, walked over to the window that looked out on Gerard Avenue, still staring at the picture, as if frozen in that position.

Michael whispered to Manny, "It's like he's in a trance."

"He's starting to get into character," Manny said. "It's an actor thing."

"Oh."

"Remember that scene in *Caddyshack*?" Manny said, referring to another one of his favorite movies of all time. "It's like when the guy tells himself, 'Be the ball.' "

"So he's trying to be the photograph?" Michael said.

"Something like that," Manny said. "He's cool, isn't he?"

Michael didn't answer, because he was thinking, weird is more like it.

This was never going to work in a million years.

18

Carlos had his own lies, separate from his brother's.

Here was one:

He had not worked at Hector's Bronx Café for a few weeks now.

Here was another:

At night, when Michael thought he was busing tables at Hector's, Carlos was working outside Yankee Stadium, scalping tickets to Yankee games, as afraid of being spotted by his brother as by the police.

And finally the Whopper, with cheese:

His boss for this new job as ticket scalper, the one who actually dealt with the broker who somehow owned the tickets, was a young man his age named Ramon Crespo.

The same Ramon who had stolen Mrs. Cora's purse.

Carlos had met him a few nights after he got laid off at Hector's. He had done nothing wrong, the manager assured him, he had been one of their best workers since his first night on the job. But business was slower than they expected, even after Yankee games, and some of the waiters had agreed to take a cut in salary rather than be the ones laid off, and so the busboys had to go.

Carlos was out of a job, at a time when he had a secret drawer full of past-due bills in the apartment.

"But I need this job," he had said to the manager, a man named Jose Guzman.

"You told me you work at the Imperial," Mr. Guzman said. "How much can a boy your age need a second job?"

"We have bills to pay at home."

"I'm sure your father will find a way to provide," Mr. Guzman said. "And if things change around here, I will be sure to call you."

You don't understand, Carlos wanted to say. I am the father, even if I'd give anything to be just a son again.

To have somebody take care of me the way I take care of Michael.

For the next few nights, he got dressed as if he were going to Hector's, his Senators cap on his head, and walked down to 158th Street instead, hanging around with boys from the neighborhood who would stand in front of Stan's Sports World. Somebody would always have a transistor radio to listen to the Yankee games, even though they would first try to guess what was happening inside when they heard the noise of the crowd, before the announcers would tell them what had happened.

One night he was listening to one of the boys on the corner tell the story of how he had cried in front of the judge in Juvenile Court, boo hoo, getting a laugh now by touching his tongue to his cheek and leaving a wet mark there, and how the nice woman judge had actually let him off.

"I wouldn't have been there at all if that stupid kid hadn't clipped me with a lucky throw."

Carlos couldn't help himself.

"He isn't stupid," he said. "And it wasn't lucky."

Ramon gave him a little nod with his chin. "How would you know?"

"That kid is my kid brother," he said.

He shouldn't have said anything, but he was in a bad mood and this Ramon, with his slicked-back hair tied into a ponytail in back, reminded him of a weasel. He was wearing a 50 Cent T-shirt and basketball shorts that were almost long enough and baggy enough to be a skirt. The purse snatcher didn't look so tough to Carlos. If he wanted it to be on, Carlos was ready to throw down with him. He even felt his fists clenching behind his back.

Ramon looked Carlos up and down, like he were some kind of item in a store window he was thinking of buying, his face almost curious.

Suddenly he laughed.

"You're right!" he said. "It wasn't a lucky throw. That boy's arm is, like, crazy."

"You don't seem too mad about it," Carlos said.

Ramon shrugged. "Easy come, easy go," he said. "Besides, I don't have to steal old ladies' purses no more, I've got myself a real job now."

Then he told Carlos and the rest of the guys on the corner about the scalper he had met at Stan's the week before, what he called the "preem-o" tickets the man had access to, how on a good night his cut of those tickets could be as much as fifty dollars.

Later on, when it was just Carlos and Ramon walking up 158th Street, Carlos on the lookout for Michael even then, even knowing Michael was home listening to the Yankee game on the radio, Ramon said, "You know what fifty bucks is in this neighborhood? Two purses sometimes, that's what."

And more than I was making at Hector's, Carlos thought.

Then he heard himself saying to the purse thief who bragged about fooling a judge in Juvenile Court, who didn't seem to be afraid of Official Persons or anything else:

"How could I get a job like yours?"

Ramon smiled a smile that reminded Carlos not of a weasel, but a cartoon shark.

"When can you start?" Ramon said.

• • •

Mr. Minaya said he had a friend who had a friend at *El Diario,* the Spanish paper in New York, who was making some calls to Havana, trying to see if there was somebody down there who would be willing to help track down Michael's birth certificate. And Mr. Minaya said he had talked to Mr. Gibbs, the ACS man, about maybe contacting the Little League in Havana, finding someone sympathetic to what Mr. Minaya called Michael's "plight."

The ACS man, meanwhile, was supposed to come to the apartment tomorrow and meet Manny's crazy uncle Timo.

Tomorrow was also the day of the Clippers' first play-off game, against the Rosedale Park Robins, to be played at Macombs Dam Park. Anthony Fierro would start in Michael's place, trying to make sure the Clippers hung in there until they got Michael back.

If they got Michael back.

"You know what's going to happen?" Michael said to Manny. "Somebody's going to come up with that stupid birth certificate of mine, but it's not going to happen until after the season's over. Wait and see."

"Well, there's a pretty great example of what my mom calls the power of positive thinking," Manny said.

They were sitting on the home team's bench at Macombs, Mr. Minaya having insisted that Michael come to practice. "They may not let you play," Mr. M had said. "But you're still a part of this team."

Problem was, Michael didn't feel like a part of the team.

"Look at it this way," Manny said. "Once you get out on the field it'll only hurt for a little while."

"How do you know?" Michael said.

"I don't," Manny said. "It just sounded like something I thought I should say." He stood up. "Come on, let's go test out the old rocket launcher, see if it's still firing on all cylinders."

"I know I've told you this before," Michael said, "but you sure can talk."

Then they were out on the field, in the bright sun, Michael on the mound, ready to go into his windup, Manny in his crouch behind the plate, all the green grass around them, and Michael was throwing and Manny was catching and saying, Wow, or Oh Boy, on just about every pitch, the way they had so many other times. Better times than these, Michael thought. Before there seemed to be something bad happening just about every single day.

He went into his high kick, tried to put everything he had into his next pitch, and did something to Manny he just had to do from time to time, when they both knew he had thrown one eighty miles per hour:

Knocked the best friend he had in the whole world on his butt. Again.

Laid him right out as if he'd run over him.

Michael took a few steps in from the mound, knowing Manny was just lying there to make it more of a show. "You okay?"

Manny's head came up first, big smile on his face. "I swear, I must have blacked out after the ball hit the glove," he said. "It was like you tried to throw one through everybody who's been busting your chops."

Michael walked all the way in to the plate, reached down with his left hand to help Manny up. "I don't know what you're talking about," he said. "That was my changeup."

"Cute," Manny said.

From behind the screen they heard a girl's voice say, "Hey. Hey, you guys."

They turned around.

Ellie.

He couldn't even remember how many days it had been since

they'd actually seen her. And now, here she was, as if they all had an appointment to meet behind the plate on this day. Now here she was, saying "you guys," but looking right at Michael, who looked right back at her and knew in that moment how much he had missed her.

Not that he was going to admit that to her. Or Manny.

Michael would wonder later why he said what he said, why he would want to hurt her feelings. Why he didn't let Manny do the talking, the way he always let Manny do the talking.

Why he would want to sound like a whole different person.

"Hey, it's Miss Gonzalez," he said. "Come to slum it up with us ordinary guys?"

Right away, Manny stepped in front of him, like he was cutting in on Michael in line, and said, "Hey, Ellie." He only paused long enough to stick an elbow into Michael's side, and say, "That was sweet," before he started walking in Ellie's direction.

She was wearing a Nike T-shirt and white jeans. Her sneakers, with a pink Nike swoosh, looked brand-new. Michael saw she had brought her baseball glove with her.

"You got time to play a little?" Manny said.

But Ellie wasn't looking at Manny or acting as if she'd even heard him. She was looking at Michael.

"You know," she said.

"Yeah."

"How?"

"They showed you on television," he said. "The other night. With your sister."

Manny said, "Okay, then, so now everybody knows who everybody else is, we can stop wearing our name tags." Manny made a motion like he was wiping sweat off his forehead. "Whoo, there's a relief."

Ellie was still ignoring him. "You're mad that I didn't tell you myself."

Michael said, "Who, me? Why would I be mad about a little thing like you lying to me?"

He still sounded like somebody else. And still didn't care. He felt like he was in some silly schoolyard fight, just with words, and wanted to beat her to the punch.

Out of the side of his mouth, Manny said, "Aw man, don't go *there*."

"I didn't lie," Ellie said. "I just didn't tell you everything. Do you tell everybody all your secrets?"

"What does that mean?" Michael said.

"What does what mean?"

"About secrets?"

"I was just saying . . ."

"It's different," Michael said. "You're his daughter."

"That's exactly why I didn't tell you."

"Blah blah blah blah blah," Manny said.

"What, you didn't think we'd like you for yourself if we knew who you really were?"

They were still talking through the fence, Ellie making no move to walk around to where they were standing behind the plate.

Like we're strangers all over again, Michael thought.

"Something like that," Ellie said.

"We liked you because we liked you," Michael said.

Another thing he'd wonder later: Why he dug in like this, like he was digging a hole with those old spikes of his into the batter's box.

"Not everybody does," she said.

"We're not everybody," Michael said.

"Boy," Manny said, still trying to lighten everything up, "you can say that again."

"You don't understand how hard it is, being his daughter," she said.

"I wish that was the worst problem I had," Michael said.

"That's not what I meant. . . ."

"It was stupid to keep it from us," Michael said.

He knew he sounded like a jerk, that he didn't even sound like himself. Carlos liked to say that his little brother would walk around the block to avoid hurting someone's feelings.

Now he was doing that to Ellie. On purpose.

"So now I'm stupid," she said. "Anything else?"

"I don't think my jerkball friend meant to call you stupid," Manny said. "Did you, jerkball friend?"

"No, he's right," Ellie said. "I think mostly I was stupid to come here today."

She didn't run away this time.

She walked.

Manny gave Michael about the meanest look he'd ever seen, then said, "Ellie, wait."

All she did was wave an arm, like, leave me alone.

She kept walking, across the basketball courts and up the hill, never once looking back.

19

No baseball.

Now, no Ellie.

The next thing to go wrong would be Uncle Timo with Mr. Gibbs tomorrow. Michael could see it now, every time he thought about it. Just because of the way things were going. Uncle Timo would slip up somehow or Mr. Gibbs would trip him up with some question he already knew the answer to, like one of Carlos's know-it-all television lawyers. And all of a sudden, Uncle Timo would be calling the ACS man "dude," and before the ACS man left the apartment he would figure out that Papi hadn't run out on Carlos and Michael. Even worse, that he had been dead for almost three whole months.

And then . . .

Michael squeezed his eyes shut, as hard as he could, taking the same walk up the hill that Ellie had just taken, Michael just having told Manny that he didn't feel like practicing today, he didn't feel like doing anything, he just wanted to go home.

When he got to 825 Gerard, he went upstairs to the empty apartment. The quiet apartment. Never had it seemed quite this empty to Michael, quite this quiet.

Never had he felt so alone.

"Hello, little one," Mrs. C said after Michael knocked on her door. "Come watch *Oprah* with me, I think she's going to give away more cars today."

Mrs. C had the same kind of recliner chair Papi had, one that

Michael sometimes had to help her out of if she'd been sitting too long. He wondered how she got up and out of it when he wasn't around to help her. Somehow, though, she managed, the way she managed to get herself up the hill to Gerard when she was on her way back from the Imperial Market, having worked out a system where she bought her supplies a little bit at a time.

On days when she saw Michael in the back alley, throwing against his pitchback, she would take him with her to the Imperial.

"It is a two-bag day, little one," she would say. "Today you must be my assistant carrier. And maybe, just maybe, there will be a little candy in it for you when we get to the checkout."

Michael knew it wasn't maybe at all, she would always let him pick out whatever kind of candy bar he wanted, Nutrageous usually.

He watched her now, moving slowly across her own living room, the room as neat and clean as always, smelling, as always, of flowers, even when Michael couldn't see new flowers anywhere.

Lately she was moving more slowly. He could see that her ankles, showing underneath her long summer dress, looked more thick and swollen than ever, as if they had been stung by bees.

Michael worried sometimes that Mrs. C would be the next person he loved to leave him, even if he could not imagine his world without her in it.

"We should write a letter to Oprah the way some of these people do," she said to Michael now. "She is always trying to take care of strangers, why can't she take care of my two boys?"

Her two boys. Michael smiled. She made him smile as easily as Manny did, almost.

"Carlos and I don't need a new car, Mrs. C," he said.

"Oprah would know what to do about all your problems," she said. "I believe she is an angel on earth."

"But not a Los Angeles Angel."

It was a small joke between them, because Mrs. C talked about angels a lot, and knew so little about baseball.

"No," she said, "I don't think your baseball Angels are much of a help to us."

Now hush, she said, *Oprah* was almost over. Michael asked if he could get a drink of water. Mrs. C said there was a pitcher of iced tea she'd just made fresh in the refrigerator, and peanut butter cookies just out of the oven on the counter. He could have a couple if he promised to eat all his supper. Michael said he didn't know what Carlos had left him for supper and Mrs. C said, forget what Carlos had left, she was going to cook him up some *paella* just the way he liked it.

Michael left her with Oprah and went into the kitchen, where the baking smells were as familiar to him as everything else in Mrs. C's world. He poured himself a glass of iced tea—orange peels swimming in it as usual—and grabbed two cookies and when he came back into the living room, she had muted her set for the beginning of the five o'clock news.

She said, "Now what's on your mind, little one? There's always something on your mind when you come here. Usually something making you sad."

He told her all about Ellie then, trying to get in all the important parts, all the way to what had just happened down at the field.

She raised an eyebrow. "So this is the girlfriend you were chasing?"

"She's not my girlfriend."

"Sounds like one to me," she said, showing him just the hint of a smile. "Or you wouldn't be so upset about this."

"She's just a girl who happens to be a friend."

It's what Manny said about Maria Cuellar all the time. What guys *had* to say.

"Whatever you say." She raised an eyebrow at him, to let him know she was playing.

"I'm just trying to figure out what I did that was so wrong," Michael said.

"You hurt her feelings for no reason, little one, that's what you did wrong. And you know it. Because you are too smart *not* to know it."

"I didn't mean to, it was the words that came out wrong."

"You called her a liar, Michael."

"I said she *told* a lie she didn't have to tell."

"Obviously she thought she did."

"She should have trusted me."

Mrs. C put out her hand now, a gesture they both knew meant she wanted Michael to help her out of the chair. He did, and she shuffled over in her summer sandals and sat down next to him on the couch. Still holding his hand.

"She is the daughter of your hero," Mrs. C said.

"But . . ."

"Hush," Mrs. C said, the same way she had said it at the end of *Oprah*. "She is the daughter of the great baseball pitcher, and that is the only way everyone here sees her, no matter where she goes or who she is with. At school. Up where you say she lives, in Riverdale was it? And at Yankee games, too. Only now she makes two friends, Michael and Manuel, who have no idea who she is, who like her for herself. And she doesn't want to give that up right away, because she likes being liked for herself. Likes feeling normal for a change. You, of all people, must be able to understand that."

Michael stared at her face, her dark eyes set in the dark, smooth skin, underneath her white hair with all the curls. They were close enough for him to smell the soap smell she gave off, as if she had just come out of one of the bubble baths she always talked about, where she would rest her weary bones at the end of the day. As old as she was, Michael could look at her sometimes and see what she must have looked like when she was young and, he was sure, beautiful.

"Okay," Michael said. "I messed up. Big time. The same way I've been messing up all over the place."

"No, you have not," she said. "It's everything that has gotten messed up *around* you, little one. But it's all going to work out, I promise you."

"Right," Michael said. "Things have been working out so great for me, no reason they should stop now."

"Don't sound so resentful, little one. You know what Grandmama Cora says about people who are resentful in this world."

Michael knew it by heart. "It's like they take poison and then hope for the other person to die."

She squeezed his hand. "For now, just take care of the things you can take care of. And this Ellie of yours is as good a place to start as any."

"I don't know how."

"Call her and apologize."

"I still don't have her number, and it's not like I can call information and ask for El Grande's house."

"Leave a note for her at the ballpark."

"They'll never give it to her."

"You don't know that until you try."

"She only shows up when her father is pitching," Michael said. "And he doesn't pitch for a few more days, and the Yankees will be out of town by then. . . ."

He started to feel himself filling up again. It was happening a lot lately, when he started to think about everything and feel like he was Chicken Little, in the bedtime story Papi used to read to him, about the sky falling.

Mrs. C knew. "Come here, little one," she said, pulling him close to her. "Let's play our game."

It was the one where he would close his eyes and see the happy endings he wanted. Where everything in his world worked out the way he wanted it to. She would make him go through his wish list, one item at a time.

"Just do the baseball parts today," she said.

"I don't feel like it today, Mrs. C."

"You can do it," she said. "I'll even start you off. We've found your birth certificate and all of a sudden you're running out to the mound at Yankee Stadium, waving to Carlos and me in our front-row seats, and we cheer along with the rest of the crowd. . . ."

Michael took it from there, holding on tight to Mrs. C, his eyes closed, the smell of her soap covering him like one of her soft blankets.

Sometimes he still felt safe.

20

Carlos met Uncle Timo for breakfast, just the two of them at Orem's Diner, three doors up from the McDonald's on 161st. The two of them went back and forth about what questions the ACS man might ask, the things Carlos said Uncle Timo absolutely had to know.

Like the two of them were studying for a test.

Carlos told Michael all about it when he came back to the apartment to change into his work clothes for the Imperial. Telling Michael he wished he could get off early from work to be there, but they needed every dollar right now.

"You think Uncle Timo knows enough about us to get by now?" Michael said.

"Fingers crossed," Carlos said. "But I have to tell you, with that guy, he's serious one minute and then acting like a total nut job the next." Carlos tapped the side of his head. "He's a little crazy up here, this one."

"We're the crazy ones," Michael said. "To think we could pull something like this off with somebody as smart as Mr. Gibbs."

"You mean somebody who probably has kids trying to scam him all the time?"

"He's going to see right through this," Michael said.

"We still have to try, Miguel. We can't be looking over our shoulders for him every day from now until my eighteenth birthday. Once he's out of the way, we can try to get your birth certificate before it's too late for it to do us any good."

Michael said, "You know what Yogi Berra used to say, right?"

"Even I know Yogi used to say a lot of things," Carlos said.

"One of his best," Michael said, "was when he said it sure gets late early around here."

Uncle Timo was supposed to arrive at the apartment at twelve-thirty, a half hour before Mr. Gibbs. Manny, who had come over to spend the morning with Michael, promised his uncle would be on time.

"He knows how important this is," Manny said.

"You sure about that?"

"Would it help if I told you to relax again?"

"No!" Michael said.

At twelve forty-five Uncle Timo still wasn't there.

Manny used the phone in the kitchen to try his cell.

No answer.

"You're probably on your way," Manny said into the receiver. "But please call when you get this."

Michael went over and sat on the windowsill, looking one way and then the other, hoping he would see Uncle Timo walking up the street before Mr. Gibbs.

All he saw was a street-cleaning truck, and some little girls from across the street playing four-square on a chalk outline on the sidewalk.

"What time is it now?" he said to Manny.

"Five minutes since the last time you asked me," Manny said.

Michael sighed and wished Carlos was around.

As soon as he went back to his perch on the windowsill, he saw Mr. Gibbs come around the corner of 158th Street.

Still no Uncle Timo.

"He's here," Michael said to Manny.

"Great."

Michael said, "What do we tell him when he asks where my father is?"

"That he's out running an errand and he'll be right back," Manny said.

There was a knock on the door. As Michael went to answer it, Manny said, "One more thing?"

"We have enough things."

Manny said, "I think it would help if you didn't look like you just broke a window."

Michael gave him a face and opened the door. Mr. Gibbs was wearing a faded short-sleeved shirt with a tiny crocodile on the front, hanging out over his pants, and the same beat-up sneakers he'd been wearing the other times Michael had seen him.

"My dad will be back any second," Michael said, not even bothering to say hello. "He had to run an errand."

He didn't move, just stood there with his hand on the doorknob. Mr. Gibbs didn't move. Finally Mr. Gibbs said, "Do you mind if I come in and wait inside?"

"Sorry," Michael said, making a sweeping gesture with his hand like he was showing him in. "Did you ever meet my friend Manny?"

"The catcher," Mr. Gibbs said.

Manny smiled, obviously pleased that Mr. Gibbs had recognized him.

At least somebody was in a good mood.

Mr. Gibbs said to Michael, "Is Carlos coming?"

Michael explained that Carlos had to work. Mr. Gibbs said he understood, and sat down. Michael, trying to remember his manners, asked if he wanted something to drink. Mr. Gibbs said he was fine for now. Then nobody said anything for what seemed like an hour to Michael until Mr. Gibbs said, "It must be great having your dad home."

"I just wish he could stay longer," Michael said.

"When does he have to go back?"

"Today or tomorrow, he's not sure."

Would Uncle Timo say that?

Shoot.

"He probably wishes you were pitching tonight."

"Not as much as I do," Michael said.

"Correction," Manny said. "Not as much as *we* do."

"On that subject," Mr. Gibbs said, "if there's anything I can do . . ."

Michael said, "Carlos keeps calling people. In Havana, I mean. But the phone calls are expensive, and always it seems that the person he's talking to isn't the person he needs to be talking to."

"I hate to say it," Mr. Gibbs said, "but in that sense, Castro's government sounds a lot like ours."

"Sometimes I think we need a miracle," Michael said.

The door opened then, and Uncle Timo walked in.

Only he wasn't Uncle Timo, at least not today, Michael could see it without his having said a word.

He knew he was staring, but he couldn't help himself.

Uncle Timo had turned himself into Papi.

21

EVEN MANNY WAS SPEECHLESS FOR A CHANGE.

Uncle Timo was wearing Papi's favorite old khaki slacks, the ones Carlos had sent home with Manny the night before, and the kind of black T-shirt their father had always seemed to be wearing when he wasn't driving. Papi's old pocket watch, the one that had belonged to their grandfather, was attached to a thick chain hanging from Uncle Timo's belt.

But it wasn't just the clothes.

In just one day Uncle Timo's beard looked as heavy as Papi's had been the day he died. And he had shaved his head into the dark crew cut Papi always wore in the summer.

Even from where he stood across the room, Michael could see the tattoo on Timo Morales's right forearm of a tocoroco, the national bird of Cuba, the feathers almost as big as the bird itself.

Just like Papi's tattoo, the one he used to joke was better than anything any NBA player had on his arm or his leg or even his neck.

Michael was wondering if it was real as Uncle Timo walked toward him with his arms stretched wide the way Papi always did when he came through the door, hugged him close, kissed the side of his face, Michael feeling a familiar scratch of beard that actually made him shiver.

I feel like I'm with a ghost, he thought.

"El ratoncito, Miguel," he said.

It meant, Mike the little mouse.

"Father," was the best Michael could do.

He even *sounds* like him, Michael thought, the words coming out in a husky voice, like the low growl of a dog.

The accent was perfect.

Uncle Timo pulled back now, winking at Michael as he did, saying, *"Silencio, no hay que gritas, no se vaya a despectar."*

Carlos must have given him Cuban expressions to use whether they made sense or not. If Mr. Gibbs did speak Cuban somehow, he was probably wondering why Michael's father was telling him not to scream and wake up the cat.

Uncle Timo turned toward Mr. Gibbs then, right hand extended toward him, saying, "How do you do, sir, I am Victor Arroyo and am here to be thanking you so much for taking an interest in my *ratoncito.*"

Papi's English, Michael thought, was better. Had been better. But Mr. Gibbs didn't know that.

The two men shook hands. As they did Mr. Gibbs said, "I speak a little Spanish, but not enough to know what that means."

"From the time he was born and made these little squeaks in his crib, Michael has been my little mouse," Uncle Timo said. "Even as I watched him grow up and start to throw a baseball like a young Sandy Koufax." He pointed a finger now at the ACS man, said, "You are the right age to have seen the great Koufax, am I correct, sir?"

"You got me," Mr. Gibbs said. "He was my favorite pitcher of all time. I grew up in Brooklyn, but I was one of the kids who kept rooting for the Dodgers after they left for Los Angeles."

"The way we Cubanos always rooted for our baseball heroes after they started leaving us for America."

The two of them standing here and chatting like old friends after knowing each other for, what, two whole minutes?

"Please have a seat, Mr. Gibbs," Uncle Timo said, gesturing toward the couch. "I will take my favorite chair, the one I have not gotten to sit in too much as of lately, and which my sons say should be condemned."

He put a little extra accent into the last word, making it come out "condemn-ED."

Mr. Gibbs took a seat on the couch. Uncle Timo gave Michael a quick wink, as if the two of them were sharing a private joke. "And what about you two? Would you care to sit down and join us, Miguelito?" Another Papi expression. "Or are the two of you just going to stand there like statues in a church?"

"I'm fine," Michael said.

"I'm good," Manny said.

Uncle Timo got right to it with Mr. Gibbs.

"I am so sorry," he said, "for somehow making you worry that I had abandoned my two boys."

"I just feel that in my job," Mr. Gibbs said, "it's better to be safe than sorry. And, believe me, the last thing we want to do at the ACS is put two more boys in the care of the city."

"Of course."

"There was a time," Mr. Gibbs said, "when we had over fifty thousand children in the system. But over the past several years, that number has dropped to under twenty thousand."

Uncle Timo sighed. "It is still a big enough crowd to fill the Madison Square Garden."

"It's why I'd rather be too nosy than not nosy enough," Mr. Gibbs said. "If I even get a whiff that two young kids may be living without a parent, no matter how well they think they're doing, I wouldn't be doing my job if I didn't check it out."

Uncle Timo's eyes locked on Michael's, the smallest of smiles on his face as he said, "We are so grateful that an Official Person like yourself took such an interest in our family, even if it has not been so much of a family lately." He nodded, as if he'd convinced himself of something, then said, "This is how we hoped America would work, people caring for other people in such a way as this."

Even Michael thought he was starting to spread it on a little thick, but he could see there was no stopping him now.

"Would anybody like some lemonade?" Michael said. "Manny and I were just going to make some when Mr. Gibbs showed up, weren't we?"

Manny said, "Right! Lemonade. Boy, I'm thirsty enough to drink a whole pitcher!"

They walked through the kitchen doors as they heard Mr. Gibbs say, "So, Mr. Arroyo . . ."

"Call me Victor, please."

"So, Victor," Mr. Gibbs said, "tell me about your brother."

Michael and Manny were standing just inside the kitchen door. Manny said, "This is *so* on."

Michael pinched Manny's arm with one hand, put a finger to his lips with the other.

"Ouch!"

"Shhhh."

Manny said, "I was just saying."

"You're always just saying," Michael whispered. "I just would appreciate it if you didn't say anything right now."

Manny couldn't help himself. "All I was trying to say . . ."

"Manny," Michael said, "just this one time, I don't want you to do play-by-play on your life."

They both listened at the door to Uncle Timo, who Michael thought was a clown when he met him, like one of the clowns that used to make him laugh at the famous Havana circus, El Guinol

Nacional. Now he was telling Mr. Gibbs a story that even Michael found himself believing, about an uncle of Michael's that did not exist:

About his brother's terrible blood sickness that was so far gone, but somehow could not kill him. About the woman his brother had lived with for years in a place called Homestead, Florida—where was *that*? Michael wondered to himself—a sweet, beautiful woman that Luis had hoped to marry once, before he took ill.

He said that her name was Julia, then actually gave Mr. Gibbs her phone number, in case he ever again had concerns about Carlos and Michael and needed to contact him immediately.

Michael poked Manny. "Who is Julia?"

"Will you *please* stop hitting me."

"Is she real?"

"Oh, now I can talk?"

Michael just stared at him, the way he did in baseball when Manny would come walking out for a chat and Michael would stare him back behind the plate.

"Julia is the name of the old girlfriend Uncle Timo told us about," Manny said. "The one from the dinner theater down there."

In the living room, Uncle Timo was saying, "I make a promise to my brother that I will be there for him until the end."

"I understand," Mr. Gibbs said.

"When I am down there, I am constantly on the phone, trying to find someone in Havana who can find a copy of Michael's birth certificate, which somehow has disappeared." There was a pause and then Uncle Timo said, "Maybe because we disappeared on the boat that night."

"It's stupid that Michael even has to be put through this, if you want my opinion," Mr. Gibbs said.

Next to Michael Manny said, "Tell me about it."

Michael made a motion like he was going to pinch him again.

"Don't come any closer," Manny said.

He cracked the door open just slightly. Uncle Timo was saying to Mr. Gibbs, ". . . I am the big stupid for making sure I did not have it in my possession before we are saying good-bye to Cuba forever and for good."

"I told Michael before you got here, and now I'll tell you," Mr. Gibbs said. "If there's anything I can do, let me know."

"Maybe if an Official Person from here called an Official Person there."

"I can't make any promises," Mr. Gibbs said. "But I'll sure give it a shot."

Uncle Timo raised his voice now and said, "I thought you two knuckleballs said you had the lemonade made already."

"Coming, Papi," Manny said.

"Papi?" Michael said.

"I want to get into the act."

"Wow," Michael said, "that doesn't sound anything like you."

Michael carried the pitcher they had put in the refrigerator. Manny brought four glasses on the kind of plastic tray you got for your food at McDonald's. Uncle Timo poured, like it was some kind of party and he was pouring wine or champagne for his guests.

Then he raised his own glass.

"To my Miguelito," he said. "May the next time we are all together be on the day when he pitches himself—and his proud papi—to the Little League World Series in Williamsport, Pennsylvania."

They all clicked glasses and drank lemonade. Uncle Timo drank his in loud gulps, then made a big show of wiping his mustache with the back of his hand, just the way Papi used to. Then, as if overcome by the emotion of this great moment, he spread his arms wide again, motioning Michael to come into them.

"My son," he said.

He put his arms around Michael and hugged him even tighter than he had when he came in, and then in a whispery voice just barely loud enough for Michael Arroyo to hear, he said, "Top *that,* dude."

22

IN HIS HEART, MICHAEL KNEW HE WASN'T GOING TO PLAY ANY MORE BASEBALL this season.

But it was all right.

Really it was.

Even if this was his one and only chance to make it to the Little League World Series. Even if it turned out he missed out on that. He told himself he would get over it, as long as he and Carlos got to stay together. And, Michael had to admit, he felt a lot better about their chances now that Uncle Timo had put on such a good show for Mr. Gibbs.

So he kept telling himself to feel good about that, mostly because he needed to feel good about something today, the first day of the play-offs for the Clippers. After all the surprises in his life lately, just about every single one of them bad, Uncle Timo turning himself into Papi the way he had, that was most definitely a good thing.

Maybe that was the way you should go through life, if you really thought about it. Maybe if you didn't expect good things to happen to you, well, when something *did,* it would seem much bigger and better than it actually was.

A few weeks ago, the only victory that would have mattered today would have been the Clippers over the Rosedale Park Robins at Macombs. Not anymore. The biggest win of the day was Uncle Timo. By a lot. Everything after this was going to be the cherry on top of the ice cream sundae that Manny was always talking about.

In Manny's view of the world, there was always another sundae coming along that needed another cherry, just because Manny believed every single day was going to be the best of his whole life.

Michael tried to remember the last time he had felt that way about stuff.

But he couldn't.

The Rosedale Park Robins were *really* good, at least when they had all their players.

The problem for them was they had played most of the season without their best player, Corey Allen. Their Michael Arroyo, as Manny referred to him. Corey Allen had managed to slice open the bottom of his foot playing soccer barefoot just a couple of days into the District 22 season. He'd had to get twenty stitches, or so Manny had heard from a friend of his who played on the Robins, and hadn't returned to his team until there were two weeks to go in the regular season, pitching well enough to get them the last slot in the play-offs.

"If he'd been healthy," Anthony Fierro was saying after infield practice at Macombs, "they'd have been good enough to fight us for the number one seed."

Manny at that moment was trying to stuff a world's record amount of bubble gum into his mouth, his right cheek already looking as if he had a baseball in there.

"Yeah," he said, "and if my mom had wheels, she'd be a bicycle."

"I was just saying," Anthony said.

Mr. Minaya said, "The great football coach Bill Parcells has a saying."

Michael looked at Manny, who rolled his eyes, just because for about the one thousandth time, Mr. Minaya had a saying that applied to whatever they happened to be talking about. Michael figured that the great Bill Parcells probably ran out of sayings eventually, but Mr. M never did.

Mr. M said, "Coach Parcells likes to say that in sports, you are what your record says you are."

"I liked our record a lot better when we had Michael," Manny said.

"We will win tonight and get young Mr. Arroyo back somehow before we play again," Mr. M said.

In your dreams, Michael thought.

And mine.

"Win one for Michael!" Manny said.

"Win one for Mike!" Anthony said.

Then all the Clippers were gathered around Michael, and chanting, "Mike! Mike! Mike!"

Almost making him feel like a real part of the team.

Right before the start of the game, Mr. M came over to where Michael was sitting, at the end of the bench, near the big duffel bag filled with their practice balls.

"I want you to coach third base tonight," Mr. M said.

Michael put a hand to his ear, as if he hadn't heard him correctly.

"Excuse me?"

"I want you to coach third."

"No way."

Mr. M grinned, "Way," he said, sounding like one of the kids on the team.

"Mr. M," he said. "You always coach third, every single game. And this isn't every single game, it's a *play-off* game."

"I know."

"Corey Allen is pitching," Michael said. "Which means every run is going to count."

"Yes, I'm aware of that," Mr. M said.

Michael looked around, to make sure nobody else could hear. "*Please* don't make me."

"You should want to coach third," Mr. M said.

"Why is that?" Michael said.

"Because coaching third is as close as you can get to the action without actually playing," Mr. M said. "And in my opinion, getting you as close to the action as possible gives us our best possible chance to win the game."

Michael could see there was no way he was going to change his mind. Once Mr. M dug in, he dug in.

"I hope you're right," Michael said.

"I am."

He was wrong.

In the bottom of the fifth, with Anthony Fierro—in Manny's words—pitching his lungs off, the game was still scoreless. Kel was on first, nobody out. Manny put a great swing on a Corey Allen fastball and drilled it up the alley in left-center, between the center fielder and the left fielder.

It looked as if the ball was going to roll all the way to the wall.

Until it didn't.

The center fielder came over and cut the ball off. By then, Michael was sure that the ball was deep enough to score Kel whether it got cut off or not. So he was sending Kel all the way, from the time he rounded second, waving his arms like he was a windmill, even as the center fielder made a perfect cutoff throw to Corey Allen himself, standing near second base.

Michael sent Kel home even though he could have held him at

third and the Clippers would have had runners on second and third, still with nobody out.

Corey Allen caught the ball and turned and threw home all in one motion, threw home as if he were throwing one of his fastballs, threw a perfect strike to the Robins' catcher, who put the tag on Kel and kept the game at 0–0.

Manny didn't take third on the throw to the plate. He hesitated as he watched the play at the plate, then must have decided that he didn't want to run himself into a double play, run the Clippers right out of the inning. So he only got to third when Chris Nourse grounded out to the Robins' second baseman, the kid making a terrific sliding stop to keep the ball from going into right field, then getting Nourse by a step at first.

Then Anthony Fierro struck out to end the inning.

Michael thought: Even with my bonehead play, Manny should have been on third. With one out, this late in the game, the Robins would have had to bring the infield in for a possible play at the plate on a ground ball, and Chris Nourse's ball would have gone past the second baseman before he even moved on it, and Manny could have walked home. . . .

Stop it, you jerk.

Mr. M always said: Never assume how things *could* have played out in baseball, or how an inning *could* have played itself out.

The truth was that Manny should have been on second and Kel on third with nobody out, and from there it would have been practically impossible for the Clippers not to be ahead 1–0. Only they weren't ahead, they were still tied.

Because of me, Michael thought.

What had he been *thinking*?

He had always taken pride in knowing the right play at any

given moment in the game. Papi had schooled him on fundamentals from the first time he had played organized baseball in Havana, back when he was seven. When he was in the outfield, he always hit the right cutoff man. When he was pitching, he backed up first base on even the most routine plays in the infield. He never took a chance on the bases, *never,* if he wasn't sure he could take an extra base.

Even as close as the backstop behind home plate was at most of the fields where they played, Manny knew Michael would always have his back on plays at the plate. Three or four times this season, there had been a bad relay throw that skipped past Manny, but Michael had been there to scoop the ball up and throw out somebody on the other team being foolish enough to take an extra base on him.

Now he had been responsible for the bonehead play of the year. The District 22 play-offs were double elimination, so the season wasn't over if the Clippers lost to the Robins. Just as good as over. Because as soon as you lost a game in the play-offs, you went into the losers' bracket—for losers like me, Michael thought as he walked slowly behind the screen to get back to the bench—and had to play another losing team the next day just to keep playing. Extra games meant extra pitchers, and the Clippers without Michael didn't have enough pitching to begin with.

Forget about making it to Williamsport.

If they lost tonight, they'd be lucky to make it to the end of the stinking week.

"Forget it," Manny said after Michael had taken what felt like a five-mile walk back to the bench and sat down with him. "We'll get 'em next inning."

Michael pulled his cap down as tight as he could over his eyes. "What makes you think so?"

"Because we are not losing to the Robins, that's what makes me think so," Manny said, using Manny logic.

"Maybe we just did." Michael tried to pull the cap down even lower over his eyes, like he wanted to use it as a mask. "I am *such* a loser!"

"Hey!" Manny said.

He reached over and tried to pull Michael's cap off his eyes and pulled it right off his head instead.

"Look at me," Manny said in a mean voice Michael almost didn't recognize.

Michael turned around, staring at his cap in Manny's hand, like he was the magician who came to school once a year and had just pulled the rabbit out of the hat.

Manny said, "If you're going to talk like a loser, go sit somewhere else, because I don't want to listen to you anymore."

Maybe there was another time when his best friend had talked to him like this, but Michael sure couldn't remember it.

"All I meant was . . ."

"All you meant was that you're feeling sorry for yourself, and you want to tell me all about it," Manny said. "I'm just telling you to stop, okay? Because it's not doing us any good. Okay?"

"Okay."

"You want to make yourself useful?" Manny said. "Figure out something that will help us win the game." He handed Michael back his cap. "Okay?"

"Okay already," Michael said.

Manny finished putting his catcher's equipment back on while Mr. M warmed up Anthony. It seemed like about five minutes later the Robins had the bases loaded with two outs.

Mr. M asked Michael, who'd been charting Anthony's pitches, how many he had thrown.

"Sixty on the nose," Michael said.

"Well then he's done, isn't he?"

"Coach," Michael said, "Corey Allen's up. You know he's their best hitter on top of being their best pitcher. Anthony only gave him a single first time up, and then he got him to fly to Teddy. He's still our best chance, even if he is right up against the pitch limit."

"Nobody pitches past sixty, Michael. Not even you."

Sixty for Mr. M, who always said he was never going to put a twelve-year-old pitcher's arm in jeopardy, was as much a magic number for him as eighty—as in miles per hour—was for Michael and Manny.

"Well, who are you going to bring in?" Michael said.

Mr. M leaned back, closed his eyes for a second, then said, "Kel. Maybe after seeing Anthony throw nothing but fastballs all game, Kel can fool Corey with a couple of those Wiffle balls he throws up there."

Mr. M sat up straight, clapped his hands together one time, as if that settled it. "Kel it is. For one batter. If he gets out of it, I'll go with Nourse in extra innings."

Mr. M called time, walked out to the mound, called all the infielders in when he got there, put his arm around Anthony's shoulders, took the ball from him. Then Michael saw Mr. M talking to Kel. Saw Kel's eyes get wide as he looked at Corey Allen in the on-deck circle. Saw Kel turn back to Mr. M and mouth the words, *No way.*

Mr. M said something else. Kel said something back. Then suddenly Kel laughed. Mr. M put Anthony at third, moved Chris Nourse to short, walked back to the bench as Kel began taking his warm-ups.

Michael asked what had been so funny that it got a laugh out of Kel.

"Manny."

"What did he say?"

Mr. M laughed now.

"Well, he didn't actually say anything."

Michael knew.

"I asked if anybody had anything they wanted to add and Manny made his, ah, famous whoopee cushion noise. The one he seems to be able to produce at will."

Michael said, "His signature move."

Then he and Mr. M both watched, neither one of them saying anything, as Kel, throwing pitches that really did seem to float up to home plate like buds blowing in the wind, finally got Corey Allen to take a huge swing at a 2-2 pitch and pop the ball to Nourse for the third out.

Inning over.

Game still 0–0.

Michael nudged Mr. M and stuck out his palm so Mr. M could give him a low five.

"*Righteous* pitching move," he said.

Mr. M said, "See, that's the thing, Michael. They're all good moves in baseball when they work."

23

Maria Cuellar walked to start the bottom of the sixth inning for the Clippers. Corey Allen was still in there pitching for the Robins, but this was it for him, even if the game kept going, six innings being all you could pitch in one game in the play-offs. If you did pitch six, you had to take one game and one day off before you could pitch again.

The Robins' coach, a loud little guy in a Yankees cap, was yelling as much now, Michael noticed, as he had when the game started, moving all his fielders around, infielders and outfielders both, as soon as Maria got down to first base.

Manny always joked that he wished you could use the kind of electric fence that people used for their dogs at Little League fields, so you could zap coaches if they went near the field for anything except making a pitching change.

The worst thing that could happen now was extra innings. But nobody on the Clips' bench, all of them with their caps turned sideways—rally cap time—was thinking about extra innings now that Maria was on base. They were thinking about ending the sucker right now.

Nate Collins, the Clippers' left fielder, bunted Maria to second.

One out.

Tommy Growney, the right fielder, grounded to second, Maria taking third on the play.

Two outs.

Their last shot at Corey Allen.

Bobby Cameron, the weakest hitter they had, at the plate.

The Robins' third baseman moved in a little. When he did, Maria said to Michael, "Any strategy here I ought to know about?"

"Soon," he said.

"How soon?"

"Right before you score the winning run."

"With *Bobby* hitting?"

"With Bobby hitting," Michael said.

Bobby was only in center tonight because the regular center fielder, Zach Frazier, was sick with some kind of summer flu. Bobby Cameron had been a decent player during the regular season, playing for the Willis Avenue Mets. But he'd stopped hitting almost as soon as All-Stars started, and now was completely clueless at the plate. He'd been up twice against Corey Allen and struck out both times on three pitches, both times making strike three easy, swinging at pitches over his head, as if he just wanted to get the at bat over with, and get back to the bench.

Now Michael could see, just by the look on Bobby Cameron's face when he looked down toward third for a sign—wanting to know if he should take a strike—that he wanted to be just about anyplace on the planet Earth except facing Corey Allen with what might be the winning run on third.

Michael knew the look, because he saw it from guys having to face him all the time.

Back when he was a pitcher, not a third-base coach.

Figure out a way to win us this game, Manny had said.

Mr. M said, "Hey," from across the field. Gave Michael the take sign that Michael was supposed to give to Bobby.

But instead of doing that, Michael called time, started walking toward the plate, motioned for Bobby to come up the line and talk to him.

He could feel everybody on the field looking at him. He gave a quick look across to Mr. M in the first-base coaching box, Mr. M giving him a look of his own. Like: What's going on here?

Michael would have told him if he could.

He was getting into the game.

The umpire said, "Let's not turn this into a chat room, boys, especially if this baby's about to go extra innings."

Even the ump didn't think Bobby had a chance to do anything against Corey Allen.

"I just want to go through the signs with him real quick," Michael said.

Michael put his hands on Bobby's shoulders, as a way of focusing him, the way grown-up coaches did when they had a conference like this. Bobby was a head smaller than he was, small and fast, a much better soccer player than he was a baseball player.

In a quiet voice Michael said, "Corey's getting tired."

Bobby said, "He'd have to be *asleep* for me to get a hit off him." He looked up at Michael and said, "And how do you know he's getting tired, by the way? You haven't had to hit against the guy."

"Trust me," Michael said. "Two people here know how tired he is. Him and me. He's dropping his arm. When he's missing, like he did with Maria, he's not just missing his spots anymore. He's missing by a lot. You know how the announcers say a pitcher's going on fumes? The guy's going on fumes. You can put your bat on him, even if it's just for a bunt."

"I can't."

"Yes, you can," Michael said.

The ump said, "Wrap it up, boys."

Michael told Bobby, "Listen up, here's what we're going to do."

"Is this Mr. M's idea?" Bobby said.

"No," Michael said. "It's mine." Then he watched Bobby walk

back to the batter's box, shaking his head, like he was being sent to his room.

Michael leaned in, made sure the Robins' third baseman wasn't listening, and told Maria what the play was, then got back into the coach's box, clapped his hands, and said, "C'mon, Bobby, let's do it!"

Corey Allen checked Maria, then went into his windup. As he did, Bobby Cameron squared to bunt. Just about every member of the Robins—and what sounded like half the neighborhood—yelled, "He's bunting!"

Their first baseman charged. Their third baseman charged. Corey Allen charged from the mound.

He didn't need to.

Bobby bunted at the ball and missed it by about two feet.

Now Corey Allen was the one shaking his head as he walked back to the mound, like he couldn't figure out what Bobby was thinking, trying some kind of squeeze play on him with two outs.

Michael leaned toward Maria and said, "Same deal."

Bobby squared again. Nobody needed to yell this time, everybody just charged the way they did the pitch before, and then watched as Bobby missed again.

Oh-and-two count.

Michael looked across at Mr. M, standing there in the first-base coach's box, arms out, palms up. Not looking at Bobby. Looking at Michael again, clearly mouthing these words:

What . . . are . . . you . . . doing?

Ignoring him, Michael took two steps toward third base, said to Maria, "Be ready to run home when he puts this one in play."

Maria was watching Corey Allen. Out of the side of her mouth she said, "*When* he puts the ball in play?"

Michael told her what he'd told Bobby Cameron: "Trust me."

Bobby squared this time before Corey Allen even went into his windup. Corey almost looked bored as he made the little rocking motion just before throwing the ball.

It wasn't until Corey's right arm started to come forward that Bobby jumped back into his regular stance the way Michael had told him to, got his bat back.

The pitch had nothing on it because Corey didn't think he had to put anything on it, he didn't even care whether or not Bobby was dumb enough to be bunting with two strikes.

Except.

Except Bobby Cameron, seeing the easiest pitch to hit he was ever going to see in his life, especially from a pitcher this good, was hitting away, putting his bat on the ball the way Michael had told him he would, slapping the ball to the left of the Robins' third baseman.

Who was coming down toward the plate as hard as he had on the first two pitches, and couldn't stop himself in time, or get his glove out in time. As the ball went past him, he looked a little bit, Michael thought, like a hockey goalie failing to make a glove save.

The ball was past him then, barely making it to the infield dirt next to third base. Maria was already across home plate when the Robins' shortstop, racing for the ball, picked it up barehanded and threw so wildly across the diamond trying to get Bobby at first—Bobby running as fast as he ever had on his little soccer legs—that Michael thought for a moment the ball might end up one-hopping the Major Deegan Expressway.

Clippers 1, Robins 0.

Game over.

Michael felt happy for everybody on the team, he really did.

And for a few seconds there at the end, when he was halfway

between third and home, running right along with Maria as she tore for the plate, watching their third baseman roll himself over on the grass so he could watch the ball slowly roll away from him, Michael almost felt as if he was in the game.

Almost.

And he had to admit to himself that it didn't stink watching the Robins' coach start yelling at everybody at once, even if nobody on the Robins had done anything wrong.

They hadn't lost the game, the Clips had just won it.

"How many times have we worked on situations like this?" His face turned into one of the big fat tomatoes Mrs. C was always bringing back from the Imperial for one of her special sauces. "How many times?"

Right, Michael thought, the old two-strike, two-out, runner-on-third, fake-squeeze-and-swing-away play.

We work on that baby all the time.

Michael walked away from the Robins' bench, across the infield, stopped at the pitcher's mound, found himself going there like it was the most natural place in the world for him to be, watched the Clippers' celebration from there. Half the guys were still around Maria. Manny, Michael couldn't help noticing, looked more excited at having a good reason to hug Maria than he was about winning the game.

The rest of the Clips were in a pig-pile over behind first base, little Bobby Cameron finally crawling out from underneath them, looking happier in that moment than Michael had ever seen him on a baseball field.

Bobby looked at Michael standing there on the mound then, pointed at him and didn't say anything, just mouthed a single word: *You.*

Michael shook his head, pointed his finger back at Bobby, mouthed these words right back at him: *No, you.*

Then he felt a hand on his shoulder and turned to see Mr. M right behind him on the mound.

"I know you don't want to hear this," Mr. M said. "And I know it could never be enough for you, Michael. But you did as much as anybody to win this game."

"Players win the game, Coach," he said. "You tell us that all the time. You tell us that it doesn't matter whether it's Little League or the Yankees, it's a players' game. Don't you?"

Mr. M said, "I do."

"Anthony won the game for us tonight by pitching the way he did. Kel pitched out of that jam against Corey Allen. Maria worked him for a walk when we needed a base runner. Then Bobby finally did something he told me he couldn't do. That was the coolest part of all, as cool as them beating those guys."

Mr. M tried to correct him. "*Us* beating those guys."

Michael grinned then and did a Manny, made his two thumbs and two index fingers into the *w* that every single member of the Clippers knew meant one thing:

Whatever.

"Okay," Mr. M said, "you got me there. But I do have one piece of information that *is* guaranteed to make you feel better. That coach over there with the other team? Mr. Bender? The one pouting like a kid who just lost his video game privileges?"

Michael turned on the mound. The Robins must have cleared away from the bench as soon as he stopped yelling at them. Now he was sitting at the end of the bench all by himself, staring at the Clippers players still celebrating on the field as if they were already going to Williamsport.

"I thought it got quieter over there all of a sudden," Michael said.

Mr. M said, "He's one of the coaches who signed the complaint about you and your birth certificate, and has been telling everybody there's no way you can be twelve."

"But he doesn't even know me," Michael said.

"We know him, though, don't we?" Mr. M said. "Him and all coaches like him."

Michael stared at the Robins' coach. "He belongs in the losers' bracket."

"Yeah, he does," Mr. M said. "And you helped put him there. So smile a little."

Michael did.

But Mr. M was right.

It *wasn't* enough.

He went over and gave Bobby a high five. And Kel. And then Maria. Manny came running at him and Michael knew what was coming next, the kind of flying chest bump the NBA players now did when you saw them being introduced before the game.

"I *knew* you'd think of something," Manny said.

"Bobby's the one who got the run home."

"Yeah, but you got the assist, bud."

Manny's mom had brought homemade chocolate chip cookies and Gatorade boxes for the snack. When everybody started to rip into the cookies, Michael turned and started walking toward the Stadium, where the Yankee game had either just started, or was about to start. By the time he crossed the Macombs' basketball courts, he could hear the PA music from inside. And could see people who had gotten caught in traffic or had just come late to the ballpark running for the turnstiles. As usual, he could feel the excitement that seemed to be coming through the Stadium's old walls, crashing right through them, even though it was just an August game against the Seattle Mariners.

This was one of those nights when he wanted to be inside even more than he usually did.

He didn't want to listen on the radio tonight. What he really wanted to do was sprint right up the hill, sprint past the security people working the turnstile at the press gate, blow right past them before they could stop him and head for the nearest entrance to the field, go all the way down to those choice seats near the field where he had spotted Ellie on television that time.

Tonight he wanted to be on the inside. Just once in his life.

One more dream just out of his reach, to go along with all the rest.

Michael didn't run anywhere. Nobody runs home to an empty apartment, he thought. Nobody runs to be alone.

He went up the hill, crossed Ruppert Place, made his way through the crowd, moved along the outside of the Stadium the way he did sometimes, dragging his hand lightly against the wall. Close enough to touch. Everybody else was rushing past him in the other direction, trying to get to their seats in time for the first pitch.

From inside, Michael could hear a woman begin to sing the national anthem.

Michael kept going toward 161st.

It was there, the corner of 161st and Ruppert, that he looked up, like this was another bad dream, not wanting to believe his eyes, and saw the two policemen walking Ramon the purse stealer toward the white van with "NYPD" written in huge blue letters on the side.

And not just Ramon.

Carlos, too.

24

Michael didn't know what to do.

He stood there, like he was frozen in place, like he was back at school and they were playing "freeze" in the yard at recess.

He didn't know whether to just run the other way, or yell out to his brother, or just walk over there and explain to the policemen that there had to be some kind of mistake.

Was Carlos being arrested?

And if that was true, what had he done to *get* arrested?

And what in the world was he doing with Ramon?

Carlos had said he was going to work at Hector's, like he did five nights a week and sometimes more, because he had told them to always call if one of the other busboys didn't show up for work. Now the tall black policeman had his hand on Carlos's shoulder. He wasn't shoving him toward the van exactly. Marching him in that direction was more like it. A smaller policeman was doing the same with Ramon the purse stealer. Michael could see Ramon talking away, the way he had talked and talked to Officer Crandall the day Michael's throw had taken him down in the outfield.

Every few steps, Michael saw, Ramon would stop and turn his head and say something, and the smaller cop would give him a push and Ramon would keep going.

Carlos didn't seem to be saying anything. Just kept his head down, with what Michael knew was his Washington Senators cap on his head. Carlos who had never done anything wrong in his life, who had never gotten a single detention in school. Carlos who worked practically all the time so he and Michael could stay together.

Now Michael stood there and wondered if these policemen were taking his brother away in some sort of portable jail.

But why?

The van, the size of a small bus, was closer to the subway station than it was to Macombs. Michael followed them toward it, keeping what he thought was a safe distance, afraid that at any moment Carlos might turn around and see him.

And what do I do if Carlos does see me? Michael thought.

He wanted to do *something* to help, it's what he thought a brother should do. He just didn't know what.

Where was Manny when he really needed him?

Michael had never paid much attention to the white van before, just knew it was always there for Yankee games, sitting there at the curb, part of the scenery on game nights the way the outside vendors were. He had never seen it arrive, was never around late enough to see when it left.

He had no idea what was inside.

He thought about going home as fast as he could, telling Mrs. C what had happened, seeing if she would know what to do, then coming right back. But then he wouldn't know if Carlos was still inside, or if they'd taken him someplace else.

He had some change in his pocket, and even thought about going to the pay phone at the bottom of the subway steps and actually calling Manny, hoping that he *could* come up with some bright idea. . . . After all, wasn't it Manny who had come up with the idea of a fake dad?

Or maybe that's what I should do, Michael thought, call my fake dad, Uncle Timo, the way kids called their real dad when they were in trouble.

An hour ago, it seemed like the worst thing that could possibly happen to him tonight was running Kel into that out at home plate against the Robins. . . .

The smaller policeman walked Ramon up some stairs and into the van. Carlos and the tall policeman stayed outside, Carlos with his head still down, the policeman pointing a finger at him and doing all the talking, Carlos just nodding his head sometimes.

Ever since Papi died, Michael and Carlos had joked to each other that they had to stay one step ahead of the law.

Not anymore.

For the first time, Michael noticed what was written on the side of the white van, in small blue letters underneath a huge picture of a badge, and the huge letters that said **NYPD:**

Prisoner Transport Trailer.

Michael waited. He had decided that if Carlos didn't come out in the next few minutes, he was going to walk over to the van, knock on the door, and ask to see his brother.

Just then, the door opened and Carlos came out, followed by the policeman.

Carlos hesitated for a second and in that moment looked straight at Michael as if he knew Michael had been there all along. Michael started to wave to his brother.

Carlos shook his head.

Michael pulled his arm down, stayed right where he was. Carlos came down the steps. The policeman followed him. Then the policeman was talking very hard to Carlos again, wagging his finger in front of his face, like he was saying, Don't ever let me catch you here again.

Carlos just kept nodding right along with him.

Then an amazing thing happened. Amazing to Michael, anyway.

The policeman shook Carlos's hand, and pointed toward River Avenue, like he was telling Carlos to go home.

Like he was letting him go.

Still Michael didn't move.

Carlos waved back at the policeman and walked toward the subway station, crossed River without looking back as Michael heard a huge cheer, what sounded like a Yankee home run cheer, from inside the Stadium.

He didn't understand what he had just seen. He didn't know what had happened to Ramon the purse stealer, and didn't care. He didn't know what he was supposed to do now.

So he started walking home, hoping that was where Carlos was going.

No jail, Michael thought.

There was another cheer from inside, as big as before. Back-to-back home runs maybe?

Michael wanted to cheer, too.

No jail.

They were in Mrs. C's apartment. She had made them both fried-egg sandwiches with crispy bacon and some kind of jalapeño cheese that was a little spicy for Michael, not that he would ever admit that in front of Mrs. C or his brother.

She was even letting them have soft drinks, Coke in those small bottles that Papi always said made the soda taste much better than plastic bottles or cans.

Carlos had been doing all the talking.

Mrs. C said she had told him when he called from what she

thought was a real police station to come knock on her door whenever he got home, even if it was the middle of the night. She was the one Carlos had called when the tall policeman—his name, according to Carlos, was Officer McRae—had told him he had to contact an adult or guardian.

That was when Officer McRae was still playing the part of what Carlos called "bad cop," acting for all the world as if Carlos was going to be arraigned as an adult in the Night Court at the Bronx County Courthouse that would be in session in a few hours. Where, Officer McRae told him, he would be given a court date and released in his own "recognizance."

"You know what that means, Miguel?"

Michael said he did, from all the times watching *Law & Order* with his brother.

"I know what you're thinking," Carlos said. "I finally ended up in one of our favorite shows."

"It's not what I was thinking," Michael said. "I was just thinking I'm glad we're here together."

Carlos told them the whole story then:

Meeting Ramon on the street after he got laid off from Hector's. Ramon telling him how much money a person could make scalping tickets if you knew how to do it right. Ramon finally talking him into it. Carlos telling himself he was only going to do it until he could find a better job.

"But why?" Michael said.

"Because I couldn't pay the bills," Carlos said, his eyes getting all red again, the way they had when Michael had run into their own apartment when he got back to 825 Gerard, run right across the room and hugged Carlos the way he hardly ever did. "Because," Carlos said, "if I paid electricity one month then I had to wait until the next month to pay the phone. Because I felt like one of those jugglers with the painted faces we used to see at El Guinol Nacional, Miguel. I tried, hombre. I really tried."

"You should have told me," Michael said. "Maybe I could have helped out."

"You never said anything," Mrs. C said.

"The man of the house isn't supposed to," Carlos said.

"Only when he is too proud," she said, wagging her finger at him the way Officer McRae had in front of the Prisoner Transport Van.

"Papi never asked anybody for help," Carlos said.

"And one day it helped kill him."

Michael didn't even realize the words were inside his head until he heard himself saying them.

Carlos whipped his head around and Michael was afraid he was going to get yelled at for saying something like that.

But his brother smiled instead. "Sometimes I think you're the older brother," Carlos said.

"Maybe that's why they think I'm too old for Little League."

"No," Carlos said. "It is because of the old soul Papi always said you had."

Michael had never understood what that meant, an old soul, just knew Papi used to say it all the time, before he would lean down and give Michael one of those kisses with his scratchy beard.

Carlos pounded his fist on Mrs. C's kitchen table. "I could have ruined everything!" he said. "Going for easy money."

Ramon, he said, had showed him the moves, how to discreetly hold up two fingers, as though making an old-fashioned peace symbol, looking for the eye contact that meant somebody was interested.

Told him to always be suspicious of any fan walking into the Stadium by himself and still seemed interested in buying two tickets, because sometimes that meant you had run into an undercover cop from the Stadium Detail.

Ramon had told Carlos that if that happened, if he even thought he had been "made," to get ready to run. And to always have the escape route he wanted to use mapped out inside his head.

Tonight it wasn't just one fan, as things turned out. It was a young couple, a man and a woman, both in Yankee home jerseys, saying they were in the upper deck, and were hoping to move a little closer to the planet Earth, if that was at all possible.

They were both from the Yankee Stadium Detail, pulled out their badges before Carlos could run or do anything, showed their badges to him just as two other plainclothes cops were grabbing Ramon about a hundred yards away.

The man and the woman then handed him over to Officer McRae, who walked him to the van.

"What happened to Ramon?" Michael said.

"What Officer McRae said was going to happen to me. They took him to Night Court. Ramon must have forgotten to tell me he'd been caught once before, and given a warning, been told exactly what would happen to him if they ever caught him again."

"Fast runner, this Ramon," Mrs. C said. "Slow learner."

"Two strikes and you're out," Michael said.

Carlos said, "Something like that."

Ramon had been taken to one part of the van, Carlos to another. Carlos told Officer McRae as much truth as he could, that his father was away and that he had been holding down two jobs and had lost one of them, then been dumb enough to listen to somebody like Ramon.

Finally, after Officer McRae felt he had scared him enough, he told Carlos he was releasing him because of what he called "officer's discretion."

"When he got me outside," Carlos said, "he told me that if he ever saw me at Yankee Stadium again, I better be handing the ticket in my pocket over to somebody at one of the turnstiles."

Carlos looked at Michael. "I am so sorry, little brother."

Michael had never seen his big brother cry, not even over Papi, but he was afraid he might now.

Mrs. C spoke before Michael could.

"Sorry for what?" she said. "Scalping is against the law. Loving your brother is not."

25

TWO NIGHTS LATER CHRIS NOURSE PITCHED THE BEST HE HAD ALL YEAR, regular season or All-Stars, and the Clippers won again, beating the Grand Concourse Condors, 5–2.

Somehow, even without Michael, the Clippers seemed to be getting on a roll.

"Since you can't pitch, we shouldn't have enough pitching," Manny said. "But right now, we have enough pitching."

Michael looked at him. "You don't just play Yogi Berra's position," he said. "You're starting to sound like him."

Nourse went the first five innings, throwing nothing but fastballs. Kel pitched the sixth, throwing anything *but* fastballs. Anthony Fierro hit a home run over the fence in dead center, a three-run job, catching a fastball from the Condors' starter right on the sweet spot. Manny wound up scoring two of their five runs and talked Nourse through every single jam.

The worst was probably in the top of the fourth. The game was still 2–2 and the Condors had the bases loaded, but then Nourse pitched his way out of it with two strikeouts. Before Michael went to coach third in the bottom of the fourth, Manny sat down next to him on the bench as he started to take off his chest guard.

"It's nice to have a pitcher who doesn't act like he might break out in a rash if we have an occasional conversation on the mound," Manny said.

Michael said, "By conversation, does that mean Chris gets to talk, too? Because I don't recall seeing his lips moving when you were out there chattering away."

Manny made a snorting sound. "There are all sorts of ways people can communicate."

"Yeah," Michael said, "but there's only one you really like."

"Which is?"

"You talk, the rest of us listen."

Anthony hit his three-run shot in the bottom of that inning and that had done it. They'd won again.

Michael stayed around after the game. Carlos was back working at Hector's for the next few nights, they'd called him because two of the waiters who had been serving as busboys were out sick. Manny had gotten permission from his mom to spend the night with Michael.

While they were eating their snack after the game, Michael thought for a second he saw Ellie watching from the top of the hill, not right above the basketball courts, more toward the corner of 161st and Ruppert. But when he went to get Manny, to see if he thought it was her, whoever it was at the top of the hill was gone.

"The Yankees don't get back from Boston until tomorrow," Manny said. "She never shows up when they don't have a game."

"And her father isn't pitching."

"Maybe you're seeing things," Manny said. "Wishful thinking, dude."

"What's that supposed to mean?"

"You know exactly what it means," Manny said. "You know you want to see her."

Kel came by, his mouth full of ice cream sandwich. "See who?"

"Nobody," Michael said, giving Manny a squinty-eyed look.

Kel said, "Michael got a sweetie?"

Michael said to Manny, "Tell him I don't have a sweetie."

Manny grinned. "Okay, I don't have a sweetie."

Now Kel grinned. "What, Maria don't count?"

"Shut up," Manny said.

When he got a line that worked for him, he stayed with it, Michael had to give him that.

He did want to see Ellie. In the worst way. Even if he would never admit that to Manny or anybody else.

He wanted to tell her he was sorry for being mean to her that day. He wanted to tell her that if he ever got to pitch another big game, he wanted her to be there to see it.

In his head, it was always the game at Yankee Stadium, the one Manny wouldn't let him talk about for fear of jinxing the Clippers, the game that would get them to Williamsport. *That* was the game he wanted Ellie to see, Michael standing wherever they would put the mound for a Little League game, bringing his own heat in the same place her father brought his. . . .

Out of all of his dreams, this was the one he liked the best, even if it seemed to be the one most out of his reach.

The way Ellie was out of his reach.

How could he get to her?

Was she still coming to watch every time her father pitched? Or did she stay away from the Stadium the way she was staying away from Michael and Manny?

Did he want to wait outside the blue barriers and call her name when she walked into the ballpark with her father?

If he did that, would she stop to talk to him, or just keep walking?

Manny always said it was much easier to figure out slugging percentages than it was to figure out girls.

Maybe, Michael thought, he could he ask the guard at Yankee Stadium to give her a message if he got over to the ballpark early enough, before the crowds began to form behind the blue barriers in the late afternoon.

Oh, right. Just walk up and hand the man a note and tell him to make sure to give it to El Grande's daughter when the two of them arrived. *If* she was with El Grande when he arrived. Like that was ever going to happen on *this* planet.

Sometimes he pictured himself taking the train up to Riverdale, but he could never figure out the next part. Ask somebody at the station for directions to El Grande's house?

There was no game for the Clippers that night. No practice. Their next game wasn't until the end of the week, Friday probably, depending on what happened with a losers' bracket game. Manny wasn't around, he'd gone into the city with his mother to see Uncle Timo in the rehearsal for what Manny called an off-off-off-off Broadway play—"If it were any more off Broadway, they'd be putting it on inside the Lincoln Tunnel," Manny said—and wouldn't be back until tonight.

They'd invited Michael to join them. Manny said it was a comedy, but Michael didn't feel much like laughing today. And he didn't need Manny and his mom telling him that things were going to work out, just wait and see.

He needed to come up with a plan.

A plan to see Ellie again.

At two-thirty, a little before the first Yankee players began to show up for a night game, he sat down at the kitchen table and wrote out the note and stuffed it in his pocket and headed for Yankee Stadium.

He didn't have a real plan yet. It was like the ghost captain said in *Pirates of the Caribbean,* when he was explaining to Captain Jack that something wasn't actually a pirate *code.*

What Michael really had was more like *guidelines.*

• • •

Sometimes, even if the Yankees weren't playing one of the top teams or their hated rival, the Red Sox, the crowd still began to form early between the players' parking lot and the players' entrance. Today was one of those days. By the time Michael made his way to the blue barrier, the fans were already six or seven deep.

He figured that the way things were going for him in his life, El Grande would already be inside the Stadium, even though he only showed up this early when it was his turn to pitch. But when he asked a boy in a Yankees cap if he'd seen El Grande yet, the boy said, "No. And I got here at two o'clock, before the manager even showed up."

"You're sure?" Michael said.

"No," the boy said. "I decided to trick the first kid who asked me."

"Sorry," Michael said.

Joe Johnson was the first Yankee to arrive after Michael got there. He wore a colorful, Hawaiian-looking shirt and baggy shorts and sandals. And dark sunglasses so big Michael thought he was worried about death rays from outer space.

The people around Michael seemed to scream in one voice:

"JOE!"

Then everybody was shouting something different.

"Joe . . . Over here, Joe . . . Sign this ball, Joe? . . . C'mon, Joe, I've been waiting all season . . . Please, Joe . . . For my son, Joe . . ."

Like these were the words to some crazy song, all the words running together. People yelling their heads off, like they were warming up for the game. Though Michael always wondered how many of the people out here had tickets to the game, and how many were like him, and never made it inside.

Michael noticed the boy next to him had disappeared. Maybe he was up at the front, reaching with the baseball and pen he'd had in his hands along with everybody else.

Michael wasn't watching Joe Johnson now. He was watching the parking lot. Lot 14. Darren Rogers, the team's rookie shortstop, an all-star already, was the next Yankee out of the lot. Then the Yankees' closer, Dave Wirth, looking like a tight end, or maybe a power forward in the NBA, six-six and at least two hundred and fifty pounds. Then the other Cuban-born player on this year's Yankees, Orlando Gaza, the little leadoff man and left fielder who was hitting .330 and leading the league in runs scored.

All his Yankee heroes.

Only today he wasn't interested in heroes. All he wanted today was a father. And not even his own—Ellie's. Maybe that was what finally changed his luck. Because five minutes later El Grande showed up.

Michael recognized the shiny black Mercedes-Benz from all the other times he had seen it pull into lot 14 in the afternoon.

El Grande had the windows of the front seat all the way down and even from where Michael stood in the middle of the blue-barrier crowd, he could hear the music from inside the car, the loud horns from what had to be the Cuban jazz the announcers said El Grande loved. Maybe it was the music of the Buena Vista Social Club. The announcers always said they were his favorite group.

"Grande!"

Somebody yelled it and then everybody turned in the direction of the Mercedes at once.

"Grande Grande Grande!"

Michael stepped back, out of the crowd, toward the Yankee souvenir store, trying to give himself some room. But room to do what? He had come here thinking he could get El Grande to give Ellie a message for him. Only now that El Grande had arrived, he wasn't sure what he would do even if he were in the front of all these people shouting El Grande's name instead of behind them.

How many times have you seen him walk past you, and the rest of these people, without even glancing in this direction? Michael thought.

He saw the Mercedes ease into one of the spots in lot 14 closest to Ruppert Place, right next to where the Yankee manager had parked. He saw the dark-tinted windows to the car go up. Saw El Grande, wearing some sort of long white shirt out of his slacks, step out of the car, carrying only his car keys.

El Grande shook hands with the two security guards posted at both sides of the open gate to the lot, then walked slowly across Ruppert, which was barely wider than a sidewalk. The people in the crowd got louder now, almost sounding desperate to get his attention.

Michael began to weave his way through the people in front of him as El Grande stopped to chat with a policeman. The people were so fixed on El Grande that they didn't notice Michael sliding this way and that, like a running back in football finding a hole in the line. Somehow Michael barely touched them. Carlos used to joke that Michael was the one who should be carrying trays through a restaurant, that he was so graceful he could carry a full glass of water through a crowded subway train without spilling a drop.

Now or never, he told himself.

Michael reached into his pocket and felt the folded piece of paper, the note to Ellie with his phone number at the bottom.

Dear Ellie,

I am sorry I hurt your feelings.

I guess I was having a bad day and took it out on you.

Please call.

Your friend (I hope)

Michael Arroyo

He got to the blue barriers as El Grande shook hands with the policeman, whom Michael saw was Officer Jasper McRae, the one with Carlos that night.

El Grande was maybe twenty yards from the entrance to the Stadium. The people around him were still yelling his nickname.

"Mr. Gonzalez!" Michael yelled, as loud as he had ever yelled in his life, trying to make himself heard, trying something different, hoping he would catch his ear.

El Grande didn't turn.

Michael felt like a swimmer doing a jackknife dive, bent over the blue barrier like he was, bent almost in half, certain if anybody touched him from behind he would fall right over.

"Mr. Gonzalez, over here, it's important!"

Knowing even as he said it that his voice was being drowned out by all the other voices, all of them trying to get El Grande Gonzalez's attention.

All of them failing.

El Grande was nearly to the entrance.

Last chance.

"El gato Misifuz!" Michael yelled now, louder than ever, his throat feeling as if it were about to explode.

The cat Misifuz. From the children's song Papi used to sing to Michael. The same one Ellie said her father loved to sing to her when she couldn't sleep.

El Grande stopped, tilted his head slightly in their direction.

"Vamos a ver quien va a tocarle a Misifuz el corazón!" Michael yelled again.

Let's see who can get to Misifuz's heart.

"Say *what*?" a voice from behind Michael said.

"What *did* the boy say just now?" another voice asked.

And finally somebody said, "Corazon? Who's he play for?" And all around Michael people laughed.

He didn't care.

El Grande was walking toward the blue barrier now, staring into it, like he was curious about something.

All around him, they started calling out to him again. But El Grande hushed them by putting a finger to his lips.

Now only Michael spoke. *"Misifuz dormido en su cama está."*

Misifuz is sleeping on his bed.

"Who is talking to me about Misifuz the cat?" El Grande asked, his eyes scanning the crowd.

Only six feet away from Michael now, just up the line. Michael smiled as if he had uncovered a secret. El Grande never answered the reporters' questions in English, Michael knew from reading the papers. He always used a translator.

But now he was asking one in English.

Michael felt as tongue-tied now as the day when he had first met El Grande's daughter. But he slowly raised his hand. The good boy in class again.

"I did," he said, his voice sounding so weak it was as if it were coming from across the street.

El Grande walked over to where Michael was standing.

From both sides of Michael the people reached toward El Grande with baseballs and caps and T-shirts and autograph books and posters and old game programs and Magic Markers.

Most of them probably thinking what Michael was thinking in this moment, that this might be as close as they ever got to El Grande Gonzalez in their lives.

El Grande put a finger to his lips again. All went silent.

Michael was certain all those close to him, El Grande included, could hear the pounding of his heart.

"El ratón puede tener corazón, para reír, para cantar, para bailar," El Grande said in a soft voice, looking down at Michael.

It was the part in the song about the mouse. Michael the mouse. What Papi used to call Michael. The little mouse in the song who loved to laugh, to sing, to dance.

Michael said the next line from the song, somehow able to get the words out, maybe because they never felt as true as they did right now.

"Las cosas son realmente malas. . . ."

Things are really bad.

El Grande nodded, then put out his right hand for Michael to shake it.

Michael did, slipping the note to him as he did.

He was about to explain who he was, why he was giving him the note, but now the words wouldn't come. And then El Grande was turning away, walking back toward the players' entrance as the people all around Michael were shouting again, El Grande not even looking at what Michael had handed him, just sticking the piece of paper in the pocket of his pants before he disappeared inside Yankee Stadium.

26

MANNY SAID THIS WAS THE WAY IT HAD TO WORK OUT, THE CLIPPERS AGAINST the Westchester South Giants in the semifinals, winner making it to the District 22 finals a week from Friday night.

The District 22 finals at *Yankee Stadium.*

Winner going from there to Williamsport for the World Series.

"Us against Justin the Jerk, basically," Manny said.

It had been four days since Michael had given his note to El Grande. Still no word from Ellie. The Yankees had played one three-game series at home, against the Royals, and then hit the road again. Two nights ago, the Clippers had made the semis by beating Harlem River Drive 8–7, Kel finally winning the game with an RBI single in the bottom of the sixth.

Now Michael and Manny were in Michael's apartment, killing time in the afternoon before the Westchester game, batting practice at Macombs not until five-thirty. They had the Yankees-Orioles game from Baltimore on the radio. The Yankees were losing again, the way they had the night before after El Grande had left the game with an ankle sprain, or something worse. Even now the announcers weren't sure. All they knew was that in the bottom of the first, after rain had delayed the start of the game for a couple of hours, he had landed awkwardly on his left leg, which collapsed underneath him. The original thought was that it was just a high sprain, but that morning, they had decided to send him back to New York to see the Yankee team doctors, and have an MRI, which would show whether he had done some ligament damage.

The bad news just never stopped, Michael thought.

Manny could always tell when Michael had stopped listening to him.

"Are you more interested in the Yankee game or our game?" he said.

"I can't be interested in both?"

"C'mon, you know you still want a piece of old Justin."

"Yeah, only I won't be playing," Michael said. "When you look at it that way, Justin and his dad have already beaten me."

Somebody on the Orioles must have belted one into the gap because John Sterling, the Yankees' radio announcer, was yelling about the ball rolling all the way to the wall. Manny reached over and turned down the sound.

"Hey!" Michael said.

Manny said, "I just want to say this one time today, and then I promise not to say it again. It should be you sticking it to Justin tonight."

There was no good answer to that, so Michael didn't say anything. There were a lot of differences between them, but this was the biggest: Manny always kept talking, whether he had something to say or not.

"I was sure they would've found it by now," Manny said.

"My birth certificate?"

"I thought that Mr. Gibbs guy was supposed to help."

"He said he'd try, and he did," Michael said. "He spoke to Carlos the other night. But all he could tell him was that he hadn't made any more progress in Havana than we had."

"Great," Manny said.

Manny asked if Michael wanted to watch *Little Big League,* one of their favorite baseball movies, saying there was just enough time before BP for them to watch it all the way to the end.

"Because if you didn't see the end, you wouldn't know if everything came out all right," Michael said. "Even if it has all the other nine thousand times we've watched it."

"It's why I love the movies, bud," Manny said. "Got to have those happy endings."

Manny pushed the tape into the VCR, came over, his face serious now, reached out and gave Michael a closed fist. Michael tapped it.

"You really are due for a happy ending one of these days," Manny said.

They heard the phone just as soon as they closed the apartment door behind them. Manny kept walking down the hall but Michael fumbled to get his key out of his pocket, thinking it might be Ellie.

He got back into the apartment on the fourth ring and picked up the receiver, out of breath, the thought of Ellie making him forget for a minute Carlos' rule about not answering the phone. Only to hear that it was Mrs. C on the other end, telling him that she'd have a plate of pasta for him and Carlos after the game if they wanted it.

Michael thanked her and hung up. When he caught up with Manny at the elevator, Manny just raised his eyebrows.

"Not her," Michael said.

Forget it, he told himself now, just do what you've always done and focus on the game. Even if it's a game you're not playing. Beat Justin the Jerk and his dad and get inside Yankee Stadium finally, even if it wasn't the way you planned.

Or dreamed.

During the regular season, some of the Clippers, and sometimes a lot of the Clippers, would show up late for batting practice. Not today. When Michael and Manny got there at five-fifteen, the whole team except for Manny was already on the field.

"Must be a big game or something," Manny said, and grabbed his catcher's mitt out of his bat bag and went to warm up Anthony Fierro, who was waiting for him over by the Clippers' bench. Anthony had pitched three innings of relief against Harlem River Drive, but had gotten three full days off now, which meant he could pretty much pitch tonight until his arm fell off, if they needed him to.

The players from Westchester South had gone to run some warm-up laps around the basketball courts. Mr. Minaya, who'd been pitching BP, had gone over to the fence and was talking on his cell phone. He put it down for a second, and yelled for the guys and Maria to get out there for infield practice as long as Westchester was still running.

"Michael, you hit them grounders," he said.

Michael took his own bat out, hit a nice one-hopper to Chris Nourse at third.

The second time around the infield he heard somebody yell, "Hey, Arroyo."

It was coming from the Westchester side. He turned and saw Justin, leaning against the small chain-link fence that protected the visiting team's bench.

Michael turned and pointed to himself.

"Yeah," Justin said.

"Hey," Michael said, not knowing what else to say to him.

"Shouldn't you be warming up by now?" Justin said. Then, in a sarcastic way he said, "Oh, my bad. I forgot you're too old to pitch in this league."

"You know I'm not," Michael said. Then added: "And so does your father."

"Prove it," Justin said. Then he smacked his forehead and said, "My bad again. You *can't* prove it, can you?"

At that point a baseball smacked into the fence, about a foot from Justin's head, the impact of it making him fall back and nearly fall down.

Michael whipped around to see where it had come from and saw Manny standing halfway between home and first.

"Oops," he said. Then he rubbed his fingers together, like a fly rubbing its wings. "Darn thing must have slipped when I was trying to throw it to third."

Justin started around the fence, like he was coming for Manny, but his father jumped up from the bench, where he'd been writing in his scorebook, and grabbed him from behind, putting him in a bear hug.

It didn't stop Justin's big mouth. "You want some of me?" he yelled across the field at Manny.

Manny turned his head and spit, then said, "You have no idea."

Justin acted like he was trying to get loose from his dad, but everybody could see he really wasn't. "What's that supposed to mean?" he yelled.

"There you have it," Manny said to Michael, ignoring Justin now. "The guy is totally clueless."

Justin's dad walked his son back to the bench, then came back and stood inside the fence, at the spot where he'd coached most of the last game his team had played against them. He pointed at Manny and said, "Why don't you worry about your own team, son? And we'll worry about ours."

Michael thought: The dad has no clue, either, if he thinks that's going to be the last word. He had a better chance of going across the street and managing the Yankees than he did getting the last word in on Manny Cabrera.

"It's like my mom says," Manny went on, for all to hear. "The rotten apple never falls far from the tree."

"All right, Manny, that's enough," Mr. Minaya said now, stuffing his cell phone into the pocket of his pants.

Manny tried to look innocent. "I was just saying."

Mr. M sighed. "Always."

Justin's dad said, "You should do a better job of controlling your players, Coach."

"I know." Mr. M smiled, but Michael knew it was like a clown smile somebody had painted on him. "Don't you just hate it when boys act like boys?"

He motioned the Clippers to come in so that Westchester could take the field. And even now, a half hour before the first pitch, you just had to breathe the air around the Clippers' bench to know how big this game was, how excited they all were, even as they all tried to act as if they were just getting ready for another game.

Papi used to say that was the best of sports, just the air around a game like this. The excitement and the nervousness in your stomach and the waiting for the umpire to say, "Play ball."

Mr. M gathered them around him now and told them what he told them before every play-off game.

"There won't be an adult here tonight who wouldn't trade places with you in a heartbeat," he said. "And that includes me."

Michael was in the back of the group. He looked across the field to the Westchester bench while their assistant coach hit ground balls to their infielders. On the other side of the fence, Justin warmed up, pitching to his dad. He was throwing hard now and every once in a while, his father would point with his mitt, the way Papi used to, as if to say, Now you're humming.

Michael couldn't take his eyes off Justin.

The guy's the biggest jerk in the world, Michael thought.

And tonight, I'd give anything to be him.

• • •

It was not the best of beginnings.

Westchester got three runs off Anthony in the top of the first.

Walk.

Single.

Home run by Justin.

It was three-zip just like that, before all the Westchester parents, and there were a lot of them, had even filled the bleachers on their side of the field.

"How many pitches did that take?" Mr. Minaya said.

He was doing what he always did when he got nervous during a game, taking off his cap and rubbing his forehead with both hands. Like he was rubbing up a baseball.

"Six," Michael said, looking down at his pitch chart.

"That many, huh?"

He put his cap back on, stood up, yelled, "Time!" He looked back at Michael and said, "Meaning, time for me to go out and lie to young Mr. Fierro a little bit."

Mr. M stayed out there until the home plate umpire came out. And whatever he said must have worked, because Anthony got the Giants out one-two-three after that.

But the damage was done.

Michael ran out to coach third base. When he got there, Justin was finishing his warm-up tosses. The catcher threw the ball down to second and the Giants whipped it around the infield. When Justin got the ball back, he rubbed it up a little, looking at Michael the whole time.

"Guess they don't have any age requirements about coaching third, though, huh?" he said.

He tried to smile, but looked more to Michael like a mean dog baring his teeth.

Michael didn't say a word. He didn't look away, stared right back at him, no change of expression. But he didn't say a word. You weren't supposed to when you weren't really in the game. And he wasn't in the game, no matter how many signs he gave, even if he had helped the Clippers win that one time.

He was just the closest spectator to the game, and both he and Justin knew it. If he said anything back to him, it was no better than somebody yelling at a player from the stands.

Kel was batting leadoff. He struck out on three pitches. Then Maria grounded weakly to second. Manny up now.

Justin's first pitch to him was right at his head, missing the bill of Manny's batting helmet by maybe an inch. Manny dove backward, out of the way. His bat somehow came flying down the third-base line toward Michael. He ended up flat on his back, helmet in the grass behind him, Manny's body half in the batter's box and half out.

Only one person on the field said anything.

"Oops," Justin said.

He rubbed his hand on the side of his pants.

"Darn thing must have slipped," he said.

The home plate umpire took off his mask and knelt down next to Manny, as Mr. M came running in from the first-base coach's box shouting, "That was on purpose!"

The umpire helped Manny sit up, then looked at Mr. M. "In retaliation for what, exactly?"

Mr. M said, "Their kid thought my kid threw a ball at him during warm-ups."

"Juan," the umpire said to Mr. M, "I can't starting warning both teams for something that happened when I was still stuck in traffic on the George Washington Bridge."

"But he threw at his *head.*"

Justin's dad was with Justin on the mound. "The pitch just got away from my son, is all," he said.

"Sure it did," Mr. M said.

Justin's dad put his arms out, shrugged, and said, "Don't you just hate it when boys act like boys?" and then walked back to his bench.

Michael handed Manny his bat after he cleaned himself off. Manny stood between third and home and stared at Justin. Justin walked off the mound a couple of steps and stared right back at him.

"Enough," the umpire said. "I mean it."

Michael was worried that Manny might still say something, or even charge Justin, and get himself thrown out of the game. Instead, he was just Manny.

"Tell me," he said, leaning close to Michael so only he could hear, "what sort of score did the Russian judge give me for my tumbling move?"

Michael couldn't help himself, despite the tension all around him.

He laughed out loud.

Justin said, "What's so stinking funny?"

They ignored him. Manny dug back in at the plate. And struck out on three straight fastballs. Michael thought Justin might have hit eighty with either one of the last two. Trying to throw a hole through the catcher's mitt.

The Giants came right back at Anthony in the top of the second and got two more runs, making it 5–0. When Mr. M went out to the mound again, those two runs in and just one out, Michael looked past them, all the way to Yankee Stadium.

Which all of a sudden seemed as far away as Williamsport, Pennsylvania.

• • •

"We gotta get to this guy," Manny said when he came off the field after the top of the second.

Manny was with Michael on the bench. The Giants' catcher had been on base when Anthony got the third out, so there was a slight delay while he put his gear back on. Michael decided to stay on the bench rather than go out to his coaching box and have Justin dog him a little more.

What did I do to become this guy's enemy? Michael kept asking himself. Become a better pitcher than him? Wasn't anybody in his league allowed to do that?

"Hellooooo," Manny said. "Did we lose radio contact there?"

"I'm sorry," Michael said. "What were you saying?"

Michael would never admit it to Manny, but sometimes he was just like background noise, like a game you had on and weren't really listening to while you did something else.

"We gotta get to this guy, that's what I was saying."

"I heard that part."

"Well, then I said the same thing in a different way, how it was time to knock some of the stinking apples out of this guy's tree, just to emphasize my point."

"Another one of your signature moves," Michael said.

"Very funny," Manny said. "Do you have any suggestions about old Justin?"

Michael said, "Our hitters could start by being a little more patient."

"Right," Manny said. "We're already down five runs to a guy pitching like . . . you. We've got five ups left to make that up or Justin the complete jerk goes to the Stadium and we go home. And you want us to be patient?"

"Pretty much."

He ran out to his spot along the third-base line then. And stood there helpless as Chris Nourse struck out, Tommy Growney rolled one back to Justin for an easy second out, and Nate Collins struck out looking.

With one out, the Giants loaded the bases in the top of the third against Anthony. Mr. M had seen enough and replaced him with Chris Nourse. "All hands on deck now," he said.

"Except for one," Michael said, holding up his left hand.

"Yeah," Mr. M said. "Ain't that the truth?"

Nourse got a strikeout. Two outs. But Justin was at the plate. Michael almost couldn't watch. He did what he did sometimes during a big moment in a Yankee game, *almost* closed his eyes, keeping them open just enough to see, as if he were watching through a slit in some closed blinds.

On the first pitch Justin, going the other way with an outside pitch, hit a screamer toward first base, the ball off his bat sounding just as loud as when he'd hit his home run in the first.

Michael opened his eyes all the way now, so he could see the ball going into the right-field corner and clearing the bases and . . .

Anthony Fierro got it.

He'd just swapped positions with Nourse and hadn't even come over to get his first baseman's mitt. Didn't matter. From where he was, playing back and off the line because Justin was a right-handed hitter, he dove toward the line, somehow knocked the ball down. Ended up on his belly, part of him in fair territory, part of him in foul.

At first he couldn't find the ball. Michael was sure Justin, coming hard down the line, was going to get there before Anthony could get up. Except here came Chris Nourse, running even harder from the pitcher's mound, covering first base the way you were supposed to but the way most pitchers hardly ever did in Little League.

Anthony managed to get to his knees, underhanding the ball to Nourse in the same motion.

Nourse hit the bag as Justin tried one of those headfirst dives coaches told you never to try at first.

The field ump, running over from the middle of the infield, had a great look at the base.

"Out!" he said.

Justin, the front of his uniform covered with dirt, jumped straight up in the air, hands grabbing for his batting helmet, taking it off his head like he planned to slam-dunk the sucker.

Michael thought: Do it.

Because it would have meant an automatic ejection.

Do it.

"Don't do it!"

Justin's dad had come running from his spot in the third-base coach's box. His voice froze Justin in midmotion.

Then Justin's dad said what everybody watching the game was thinking in that moment:

"It's not worth it. We've already got them beat."

Like he was slapping everybody on the Clippers right across the face.

Michael looked at Justin, wondering if he even listened to his father.

Only Justin wasn't looking at his father now.

He was looking past him, more toward home plate, helmet still over his head, holding it like it was some kind of trophy.

The Clippers infielders, suddenly frozen themselves, were looking in the same direction.

Mr. M was standing to Michael's left, blocking his view. But across the field, Michael could see all the Westchester fans standing now, some of them pointing.

Michael got around Mr. M, moved out to the fence in front of the Clippers' bench, saw what everybody else saw: The parade of people coming around the screen behind home plate.

Led by a man on crutches, his ankle in one of those big, soft casts.

El Grande.

His daughter right beside him.

27

It wasn't just El Grande and Ellie.

Carlos was a couple of steps behind, walking with Mr. Gibbs of ACS. And another man Michael didn't recognize, but one who had Official Person written all over him.

All of them walking straight for Michael.

Michael knew he couldn't have moved even if he'd tried. So he stayed right where he was, just inside the fence, about even with first base. El Grande—moving pretty well on his crutches, Michael thought, as graceful with them as he was on the mound—stopped a few feet in front of Michael, Michael feeling as if he were towering over him the way he had at the blue barrier outside Yankee Stadium.

"So," El Grande said, "you are the one who has been making my daughter so miserable lately."

He took his time with *miserable,* breaking the word up into four pieces.

Michael looked at Ellie and said, "I didn't mean to."

She smiled that smile at him. "I know," she said.

Then Michael looked at his brother. "Carlos . . . I don't understand. . . ."

Carlos smiled. "Let them tell you."

"Show you, he means," El Grande said.

"Give it to him," he said to his daughter.

From behind her back, she produced the envelope, handed it to Michael.

"I believe you have been looking for this," she said.

"Open it, Miguel," Carlos said.

Michael did. At the top of the thick piece of paper were these words in bold, black type: **Cuban Ministry of Foreign Affairs.**

Underneath was this:

Certificate of Birth.

And underneath *that* was his name, Michael Victor Arroyo, and the date of his birth, and at the bottom was the signature that he knew was his father's.

Michael looked at Ellie. "This . . . it's real?"

"It's real," she said.

The man Michael didn't recognize stepped forward now, put out his hand. Michael shook it. "Son," he said, "my name is Steve Kain. I'm the chief executive officer of Little League baseball, in Williamsport, Pennsylvania."

Michael said, "Nice to meet you, sir."

"I just want to tell you I'm sorry I didn't know about your predicament sooner," Mr. Kain said. "We want our best players on the field, not the sidelines." Mr. Kain gave a quick look over his shoulder, in the general direction of the Giants' bench. And Justin's dad. "Especially when they are the age they say they are."

Michael said, "I still don't understand. . . ."

Then: "How?"

The adults looked at one another, like each one was waiting for the other to say something.

It was Ellie who did the talking, for all of them.

"I don't have time to tell you the whole story now. But basically, my father gave me your note. That same day, I got a call from Manny. He told me everything."

"It was nothing, really," Manny said.

Michael turned around. Manny was right behind him. Of course. Had his back, just like always.

Michael said, "You got her number?"

"I'd tell you how," Manny said. "But I'd have to kill you."

Michael looked down at the birth certificate again. It was shaking in his hand, like a leaf in a strong wind. He looked up at El Grande.

"You did this, sir?"

"Let's just say I still know some people in Havana," he said.

"Who know some people," Mr. Kain said.

"Long story short?" Mr. Gibbs said. "Here we are."

"Now," El Grande said to Michael, "are you going to be standing here talking all night, or are you going to warm up?"

Michael didn't even have his spikes with him.

Carlos pulled them out of the bag he was holding. "Got 'em right here, little brother," he said.

He handed Michael the spikes. Michael handed him the birth certificate.

As Justin's dad came running over, saying, "Now just wait a second here."

Michael was sitting on the ground next to Manny, trying to get his hands to stop shaking long enough to tie the stupid laces on his spikes.

Justin's dad was on the other side of the fence, the field side, and seemed to be talking to them as a group: El Grande, Mr. Kain, Mr. Gibbs. Mr. Minaya, too.

"You can't just send that kid into the middle of the game," Justin's dad said.

Mr. Kain was the one smiling now. "Sure I can," he said.

He stared at Justin's dad for what felt like an hour and then said, "You're the one who did this to this boy?"

"It wasn't just me. . . ."

"You wrote the letter," Mr. Kain said. "Didn't you?"

"I was just trying to make sure the rules were enforced." His face was redder now than even a Little League baseball game seemed to make it. "I didn't want us to get into another Danny Almonte situation. . . ."

"Big of you," Mr. Kain said.

Michael thought the head of Little League was looking at Justin's dad like something he just noticed on the bottom of his shoe.

Michael said to Manny, "You could have at least told me you talked to her."

"I didn't want to spoil the movie," he said.

Manny stood up then, pulled Michael up with him.

"Now shut up and pitch," he said.

By the time Michael had warmed up, there were two outs in the bottom of the third, nobody on for the Clippers. Bobby Cameron was due up.

"Listen," Mr. M was saying to the players he'd gathered around him behind the bench, "somebody's gonna have to come out for Michael to go in. Any volunteers?"

Every member of the Clippers raised a hand.

Except for one.

Manny.

He shrugged at Michael. "You need me," he said.

"I need a batter here," the ump said.

Nobody on the Clippers moved. All those arms still in the air, willing to give up their spot for Michael.

"Well, that narrows it down," Mr. M said.

Bobby Cameron said, "Let him go in for me, Coach. Right here." He looked at Michael and said, "Mike already got me my swing."

He put out a fist and Michael tapped it with his own.

Mr. M said, "You bring your bat, Arroyo?"

"Always," Michael said.

He wanted to run to the plate to get his hacks off Justin. But he made himself walk instead, like he had all day.

Digging in, he remembered what Justin had done to Manny with two out and nobody on in the first, and reminded himself to stay loose. Don't forget you're facing a loose cannon, he thought.

Somehow Justin still had that smirk-face going for him. Like he was telling everybody that his attitude about this game wasn't going to change just because Michael was in it.

Michael took a fastball for strike one.

Then two balls, the second one inside and tight, backing Michael off the plate.

He's trying to set me up, Michael thought.

He was.

Justin tried to throw Michael his very best fastball now, his number one, daring Michael, just off the bench, to catch up with it.

But Michael was ready.

Michael was *on* it.

He made sure not to overswing. Like he was making Justin's power work for him. The pitch was a little bit toward the outside corner and Michael went with it all the way, lacing it up the alley between the center fielder and left fielder.

By the time the ball made its way back to the infield, Michael was on third with a stand-up triple.

When Kel singled cleanly to center, Michael could have walked home. Kel got thrown out stealing to end the inning.

No matter.

They were on the board.

Top of the fourth.

Michael stood on the mound, ball in his left hand again, rolling it around in his palm like it was his lucky charm, as the Giants' second baseman dug in to face him. Not feeling anything like the season might be over in a few innings.

Feeling like it was just getting started.

Manny put down one finger.

Michael went into his windup, his El Grande motion, burned in strike one, the Giants' second baseman taking all the way.

Yeah.

He overthrew the next two pitches, like he wanted to throw both of them a-*hundred*-and-eighty. One of them nearly went over Manny's head. But then he came back to strike the kid out. Struck out the side finally. As he sprinted off the mound, he saw Ellie jump up from her seat in the first row of the stands. Then he couldn't help himself, he looked at El Grande to see if he'd gotten any reaction out of him.

The great man was slowly nodding in approval.

Oh yeah.

Whether Justin was shaken now that Michael was in the game, or whether the Clippers had rediscovered their confidence, they got two more runs off Justin in the bottom of the fourth. He walked both Manny and Anthony with one out, and then Chris Nourse doubled them both home.

"I'm telling you, we're in his head now," Manny said after the inning, still out of breath. Then he grinned at Michael. "And, boy, is there a lot of room up there."

Michael, overthrowing again, too excited now that the Clips were back in the game, walked the leadoff man to start the Giants' fifth. The next guy, their right fielder, tried to sneak a bunt toward third that was half sacrifice bunt and half trying to bunt for a base hit. Manny didn't even think about yelling "First base," which would have been telling Michael to go for the sure out. Just watched as Michael barehanded the ball over by the line, planted, and threw a perfect strike to Kel covering second.

When Kel brought the ball back to him at the mound, he took his hand out of his glove, flexed it a couple of times, said, "Okay, that hurt."

"Sorry," Michael said.

"We're cool," Kel said. "We're gonna win this sucker, right?"

"Sounds like a plan," Michael said.

Two more strikeouts to end the inning. When they all got to the bench, Manny gathered everybody around him, the way Mr. M had when he asked for a volunteer to sit out when Michael went into the game.

"Let's win this right here," he said.

Kel said, "Sounds like a plan."

"Right here, right now," Maria said.

It started with a Nate Collins single to left. Now Zach Frazier, bunting on his own, tried to put one down the first-base line. Justin was all over it the way Michael had just been. Maybe that play was still in his head. Maybe he wanted to show he could get the guy at second the way Michael just had. Only he rushed the throw, and the ball sailed over the shortstop's head and into center field, and if the center fielder hadn't been backing the play up, the way you're supposed to, the Clippers would have gotten back to within 5–4 right there.

Justin paced around on the mound, talking to himself in a too-loud voice, like he was broadcasting himself over a PA system.

"You *jerk*!" he yelled.

Manny poked Michael, who was standing in the on-deck circle.

"Finally he gets it," Manny said.

Second and third, nobody out.

Michael coming to bat.

Justin's dad called time and came out to the mound. Justin finally lowered his voice, but Michael could see the two of them arguing, not able to decide who looked angrier.

Or whose head looked more likely to explode.

The only thing Michael heard before the umpire broke up the father-son chat was this:

"I know how to pitch!"

"Really? Somebody else must have put those guys on base."

"Whatever, Dad!"

Michael stood there at the plate, taking it all in, waiting for them to finish.

Michael hated all the little rituals big-league batters had when they got ready to hit, ones that he saw guys in Little League imitating all the time. When Manny did it, he wanted to laugh, just because he knew it was for show, because so much of Manny was show. But Michael wanted to groan when he'd see guys playing with their batting gloves and putting out a hand to the umpire, like telling him to wait, while they dug in. Then adjusting their helmets one last time, like they were football running backs about to carry the ball into the line. For one thing, he didn't even wear batting gloves, he thought the coolest guys in the big leagues were the few who still didn't.

But he wanted to make Justin wait, see if he could rattle him just a minute more. So he bent down, picked up some dirt, rubbed it in his hands, then regripped his bat.

Then he took his stance, not looking at Justin until the last possible moment, at which point he felt like he was watching a cartoon and could actually see smoke coming out of his ears, Justin was that mad.

Ball one wasn't even close to being a strike. Way outside.

Ball two was up in Michael's eyes.

Michael took a deep breath.

Practice what you preach now, Michael told himself.

Patience.

Then it was completely quiet for him. That place he got to on the mound where he couldn't hear a thing.

Just him and the ball.

Justin rocked into his motion.

The next sound Michael or anybody else heard in Macombs Dam Park was the ping of his TPX bat making contact with the ball.

He pulled a line drive over the first baseman's head, the kid not even having time to get his glove up until the ball was past him and rolling toward the right-field corner.

By the time their right fielder picked it up, Nate had scored easily.

The right fielder made a good relay throw, and the second baseman made a nice throw to the plate, but they had no shot at getting Zach.

Clippers 5, Giants 5. Still nobody out.

Michael took third on the throw to the plate. When he got there, he looked over at Ellie. She gave him the kind of underhanded first pump Tiger Woods was famous for. Michael just nodded. Papi always said: Act like you've done it before.

Justin, his control still shaky, walked Kel on five pitches. But to his credit, he gathered himself then and struck out Maria, Kel stealing second on strike three.

Michael was still on third. The game was still tied.

Manny up.

Michael had to put a hand over his mouth, because he didn't want anybody to see him smiling at a time like this. But he couldn't help it as he watched his friend go through all his little routines. Tightening the Velcro on both his batting gloves. Taking his helmet off as he wiped what Michael was pretty sure was imaginary sweat off his forehead. Looking over to the Clippers' stands as he did. Then over at the Giants' bench. Finally at Justin the Jerk.

Michael watched all this and knew exactly what Manny was thinking. And what he was thinking was that he was in heaven.

It was all about him now, and he was playing the scene for all it was worth, like he was Uncle Timo.

He got his bat back and gave one quick look toward third. Not to Mr. M. Not looking for any kind of sign. At Michael.

Manny winked.

Then he lined the first pitch he saw from Justin up the middle so hard it nearly took Justin's head off.

Clippers 6, Giants 5.

"Three outs away," Manny said after Anthony lined out to short to end the inning, the game still at 6–5.

"Shut up and catch," Michael said as Manny finished putting his catcher's gear on. Bobby Cameron had offered to warm up Michael, but he said he'd wait. When Manny had to, he could get his shin guards, chest protector, and mask back on so fast, you felt like you were watching one of those Nascar pit stops.

Manny ignored Michael, nodding at the Stadium across the way instead.

"Three outs and we are *there*," he said.

"Manny," Michael said. "We've had a deal all summer about talking about . . . that. So when I say shut up, I mean shut up."

Manny said, "I was just saying . . ."

"Don't be saying anything," Michael said. "About how many outs. About anything. The baseball gods you're always telling me about? They're hanging on every word right now."

"You're always stifling me," Manny said, popping up off the bench, ready to go.

"I wish," Michael said.

Michael ran out to the mound, held up four fingers to Manny. Four pitches. All he would need to get warm. When he was finished Manny threw down to Kel at second.

Michael watched his teammates throw the ball around the infield and thought:

Three innings ago I was done for the season and now . . .

Nah, he wasn't even going to think about how close they were. Just pitch, he told himself. The Giants were at the bottom of their order, Mr. M had showed him in the scorebook, as if Michael required some kind of written proof. Number eight hitter, number nine, leadoff man. It meant they would have to get two guys on for Justin to even get another at bat.

The first batter was their right fielder, a short kid with long curly hair coming out of the back of his helmet. With two strikes, it was almost as if he closed his eyes on Michael's fastball, somehow getting a bat on it, a slow roller past the mound, right at Maria. She had more time than she thought to make a play, but tried to barehand the ball instead of gloving it. She dropped it on the first try, panicked when she finally picked it up, threw wildly past Anthony Fierro. The ball rolled to the fence behind him. Runner on second.

Ninth batter now. Their second baseman. Michael's height, which meant tall for a second baseman in Little League. Big swing, Michael remembered. They must have had him in the nine spot to give them some pop at the bottom of the order. He'd hit a shot earlier in the game off Anthony that Nate had made a great running catch on. It didn't stop Mr. M from yelling, "Number nine hitter," from the bench. Michael loved Mr. M but he always hated when coaches did that—and they did it all the time in Little League—because it was usually their way of saying, "This guy can't hit." Every time one of them did it, Michael couldn't help himself, he found himself looking at the batter's face, knowing how bad it made the kid feel.

Justin's dad had the big guy square to bunt, maybe figuring his best chance to tie the game was to get the runner on second over to third, even if he had to sacrifice an out to do it.

The kid bunted the first pitch, but much too hard, between Maria and Anthony. Maria started for it. So did Anthony. Then both of them stopped at the same moment, thinking the other was going to get it.

By the time Maria picked it up, it had died in the infield grass short of the dirt and everybody was safe.

First and third, nobody out.

Michael never showed anybody up on the field, ever, no matter how badly they'd messed up. But he was hot now, really hot. They were so close. He walked off the mound toward second base, trying to look calm, rubbed the ball up hard. Took a deep breath.

"Corazón," he said to himself in a soft voice.

Heart.

Then turned back around to see Manny walking toward the mound. Even though Manny knew how much Michael hated conferences on the mound. But it was too late to stop him now.

When Manny got to Michael he said, "I've got a plan, case you're interested."

"Shoot."

"Nah," he said. "We can't shoot Maria, she's too cute."

"Jokes?" Michael said. "Even *now*?"

"Strike one, strike two, strike three, that's my plan," he said to Michael, handing him the ball.

He threw strike one. High heat. The kid on first stole second, Manny not even risking a throw down. Michael didn't sweat it, though. He could see the leadoff man had no shot at his fastball. Strike three, he knew when he released it, was the hardest pitch he'd thrown all night. Manny stepped out in front of the plate, checked the runners, zipped the ball back to Michael, and said, "Eight-zero, case you're interested."

Michael didn't have to be told.

He threw three more pretty much like that one past the next hitter. Two outs now, Justin coming to the plate. Like Manny had told him in the apartment this morning, this was the way things were supposed to work out. Michael looked around. Everybody in the bleachers behind the Clippers' bench was standing. Ellie, the quiet girl, the shy girl, put two fingers in her mouth and let out a whistle that was louder than a crossing guard's.

It made him put his glove in front of his face and smile. He almost felt like laughing, that's how happy the sight of her made him feel, even knowing there was still work to be done, one more out to get.

Michael was where he was supposed to be finally.

It was him against Justin and maybe him against all the other people who didn't want him to be here, or across the street ever, or even in Williamsport.

Michael knew the game wasn't over yet. Knew enough about

sports to know that getting Justin out was no sure thing. He'd already seen how fast things could go wrong earlier in the inning. But he was fine with all of it. Because this was the way it was supposed to be, the way it was *always* supposed to be:

His best against the other guy's.

He checked the runners, even though he knew they weren't going anywhere. Then he blew strike one past Justin, who was so late with his swing Michael thought he was trying to get a head start on strike two.

Manny didn't come out of his crouch, just got it back to Michael fast, the way Michael liked when he was going good. And he was going good now.

He let it rip.

Strike two.

One strike away.

He thought for maybe one second about wasting the next one, getting Justin to chase it. But why wait? He'd waited long enough. All he'd been doing for a long time was waiting for things to happen *to* him. Only now the ball was back in his hand. He allowed himself a quick look over to the stands again. Looking at El Grande this time.

Michael saw him nod.

He took a deep breath, went into his windup, kicked his right leg toward the sky, and one last time let the ball fly.

Pure heat.

Ball game over.

They were going to the Stadium. But first here came Manny, running toward Michael, helmet gone, mask gone, as happy as Michael had ever seen him as he jumped into Michael's arms, nearly knocking him over.

Then the rest of the Clippers came running from all corners of

Macombs Dam Park, and Ellie was out there with them, and Carlos. And just for one moment, Michael closed his eyes, like he was taking a picture of it all.

This wasn't his whole dream.

But he had to admit:

It would sure do for now.

28

He stood outside the Stadium at five in the afternoon, the way he had so many other times. Only this wasn't all those other times.

Today Michael was going inside.

Manny and Ellie were with him. So was El Grande, who had stayed behind when the Yankees went on their West Coast trip so he could continue to rehab his ankle.

No blue barriers today, Michael noticed, because anybody who showed up could go inside for free and watch the Clippers play Fordham Road in the District 22 finals.

Carlos was on his way from Manhattan, with Mr. Gibbs. Mr. Gibbs: Who had turned out to be another one of their heroes. Who the day after the Westchester South game had come to the apartment at 825 Gerard with Mrs. Cora and told them he knew about Papi. Told them that Mrs. Cora had gotten his phone number the day after Carlos had been picked up for scalping, and how he had come to her apartment, and she had told him the whole story, told him she was worried for the first time that things might not work out all right for her boys. Mrs. C had begged Mr. Gibbs to give her temporary custody until Carlos turned eighteen in late September.

But Gibbs had a better idea. He said he would start the paperwork that would give *him* temporary custody, knowing that the way things worked in what he called Red Tape City, Carlos would turn eighteen by the time the paperwork ever made it out of ACS.

But there was one condition. Carlos had to become an intern in the ACS's Bronx office and work as Mr. Gibbs' assistant until he turned eighteen at the end of September. And, Mr. Gibbs said, if he wanted to stay on the job after that, he could.

That day in the apartment, Mr. Gibbs had said to them, "You boys have quite an angel in Mrs. Cora, I hope you know that."

She put out her arms then and took Michael and Carlos into them with room to spare and said, "I told you about angels."

Carlos and Mr. Gibbs said they would pick up Mrs. Cora on their way to the ballpark, since she had informed them that she had no intention of missing a night like this for her baseball boy.

And now that boy was about to enter the stuff of his dreams.

El Grande was off his crutches by now, but still in a soft cast. Just to be on the safe side, he said. He'd replaced the crutches with what Michael thought was a pretty fancy cane. Which he used now to tap Michael on his shoulder, like he was knighting him in one of the Knights-of-the-Round-Table stories Michael loved when he was little.

"It's much better inside," he said. "The Yankee Stadium."

He always called it that: The Yankee Stadium.

"Are you ready?" Ellie said.

Manny, of course, answered for both of them.

"Are you kidding?" he said. "We were *born* ready."

Ellie went through the turnstiles first, blowing a kiss at the man who worked the players' entrance for Yankee games. Michael went next, then Manny. Then El Grande, already telling his daughter to slow down, so that her injured daddy could keep up.

Ellie led them through a doorway on their right, down some stairs, taking the steps two at a time. Michael thinking: She looks as comfortable here as she would in her own house.

When they were all at the bottom of the stairs and through another doorway, Ellie pointed at the ground. "Check this out," she said.

On the cement floor was a blue line that shot out to their right, a red line going off in the opposite direction.

"The blue takes you to the Yankees," she said. "The red to the other team's clubhouse."

El Grande said to Michael and Manny, "Follow the blue. Tonight you dress where the Yankees dress."

Manny smiled, put his hands together, looked up. "Okay, Lord, you can take me now."

"Before you even play the game?" Ellie said.

"Well," Manny said, "you make a good point." Manny looked heavenward again and said, "Check you later."

They followed the blue. Followed Ellie in her white long-sleeved shirt and rose-colored jeans, Michael and Manny nearly having to run to keep up with her.

El Grande had given up trying to tell her to slow down.

Ellie led them down a long, narrow corridor, pointing out what she said was the media dining room on her left. All of them still following the bright blue line.

Manny whispered to Michael, "You think this is what Alice in Wonderland felt like?"

Michael said, "I was thinking over the rainbow myself."

They came into an open area. Ellie hooked a thumb at the door to her right. "Back entrance to the manager's office," she said.

"Right," Manny said. "I knew that."

They took another right. There was a door in front of them with a plaque on it that said, "Pete Sheehy Memorial Clubhouse."

Michael said, "Who is Pete Sheehy?"

From behind them, they could hear the click-click-click of El Grande's cane on the cement floor as he caught up with them.

"Mr. Pete Sheehy," he said, "is a clubhouse man who they say was going all the way back to the great Babe Ruth himself."

"I have read a lot about the Yankees," Michael said. "I guess I must have missed him."

El Grande said, "He is just one of many, many ghosts here." He smiled. "It is one of the first things they tell you about the Yankee Stadium. About its ghosts."

"You think they'll be here for a Little League game?" Manny said.

"Not just here," El Grande said, "but smiling."

Then he opened the door to the Yankee clubhouse.

He showed them his locker, right around the corner from the manager's office. His locker having some kind of plaster replica of the top of the Stadium on it the way they all did. El Grande walked them across the thickest rug Michael had ever seen in his life, or felt underneath his feet, and showed them the trainer's room, and opposite that, the players' lounge, with its huge television screen and soft-looking sofas and even a couple of recliner chairs that would have probably gotten Papi more excited than anything in the place.

This place.

The Yankee Stadium.

"Only players allowed in here," El Grande said.

"That mean us?" Manny said.

"Tonight it does," El Grande said.

They went back into the main clubhouse. Michael noticed some gear he knew belonged to some of the Clippers in front of lockers across from El Grande's. He recognized Maria's bag, and Anthony's. Kel's.

All Michael had with him was his bat bag and a small gym bag with his spikes in it. He said to El Grande, "Which locker should I use?"

"Mine," he was told.

When he'd put on his spikes—in record time—Ellie said, "You guys ready to see the field?"

"Oh yeah!" Manny said.

They walked back through the door to the Pete Sheehy Memorial Clubhouse. Across the way was the runway leading to the Yankee dugout, Ellie said. Above the entrance was a sign that read this way:

I want to thank the Good Lord for making me a Yankee.
Joe DiMaggio

El Grande put a hand on his daughter's shoulder and said in her ear, "Let Michael go first."

Michael took a deep breath. Like he did sometimes before he delivered the next pitch. Then he walked down the runway and up the dugout steps and the next thing he saw was all the blue of Yankee Stadium, and grass, an ocean of green grass, greener than anything he had ever seen in his life.

He saw the temporary fences they had put up in the outfield for tonight's game, and the way they'd moved up home plate, putting a Little League screen behind it; saw how they'd reshaped the field so that the Clippers and Fordham Road could use the regular infield, just putting the bases closer together; and how they'd cut down the regular pitcher's mound to make it conform to Little League standards.

Nobody cared. It was still Yankee Stadium. Like a field within the field.

"Don't worry about my mound," El Grande had said in the clubhouse, telling him about the changes in the field. "The groundskeepers will build it back tomorrow, as good as new."

Michael saw all the outfield signs he had only seen on television. Saw the retired numbers out behind the left-field wall and saw the place next to that, Monument Park, that he had only seen in pictures, where they had the monuments for people like Babe Ruth and Lou Gehrig and Joe DiMaggio and Mickey Mantle.

Maria and Anthony and Kel had stopped playing catch off to his right, and were watching Michael now as he looked around the Stadium.

"It's so . . . big," he said to El Grande.

Best he could do.

El Grande smiled and said, "I said the same thing the first time."

Suddenly Manny just flopped down on his back, started flapping his arms like he was trying to make a snow angel in the green grass of Yankee Stadium.

"*Oh* yeah!" he said, even louder, and with more feeling, than before.

Ellie said to Michael, "He's crazy, you know that, right?"

Michael dropped his bat bag and just pointed to left field, then center, then right.

"*This* is crazy," he said.

Pretty soon the rest of the Clippers had shown up. He saw people beginning to take their seats, filling up the ground-level seats behind home plate first, then spreading out all the way down the first- and third-base lines. When Michael began to loosen up with Manny, he saw Mr. Gibbs and Carlos helping Mrs. C down the stairs behind the plate.

She waved at Michael with her green purse.

He waved back.

Almost game time now. Michael heard them testing the public address system, the one he had only ever heard from outside. He heard the famous voice of the Yankees' PA announcer, welcoming everybody to the District 22 finals, then asking them to rise for the national anthem. When the anthem was over, the announcer introduced the players and coaches from both teams, Fordham Road first, lining up along the third-base line the way the players did on Opening Day, or before play-off games in the big leagues.

Then it was the Clippers' turn.

"Batting second for the Clippers and pitching," the famous voice said, "number thirty-three, Michael Arroyo."

Manny's name was called next. He ran out and stood next to Michael and said, "This is the kind of ending I like in the movies."

"This isn't the end of the movie," Michael said. "We've still got a game to play."

Manny said, "Oh, *baby*!"

Anthony was introduced then, then Chris Nourse, then Tommy Growney. After Tommy ran past them and slapped them both five, Michael tapped Manny on the shoulder. Manny turned around, still smiling, just because he hadn't stopped since they'd gotten inside.

"Hey, Man," Michael said, feeling his voice start to crack as he did.

"Yeah, dude?"

"Thanks for everything."

"Shut up," Manny said.

The Clippers were the home team, so they took the field first. The PA announcer introduced the Yankee owner, who Mr. M had told them was going to throw out the first pitch.

When the owner, bigger in person than Michael had imagined him, the way everything seemed to be bigger inside here, got to the temporary mound, Michael handed him the ball.

"El Grande told me about everything that's happened to you,

son," the owner said. He looked as stern to Michael as he did when he was being interviewed on TV. But then he smiled. "I just want you to know we expect to see a lot more of you from now on."

"Yes sir," Michael said.

Best he could do.

The owner threw a strike to Manny, waved to everybody, and jogged off the field. Michael took his warm-ups. When he was done, Manny threw down to Kel. The Clippers threw it around. Business as usual.

Yeah, right.

The umpire yelled, "Play ball!"

Michael turned his back to the plate, rubbing the brand-new game ball up. As he did so, he saw a subway train, a number 4 probably, rumble by, past the opening in right-center Michael had only ever seen from River Avenue.

The sound of the train was much quieter in here.

He thought of all the ghosts El Grande had talked about now, the ones who were supposed to be smiling tonight as they watched him, knowing those ghosts had been joined by one more tonight:

His father.

Heard his father saying, *Now* you're pitching.

Michael turned back around. The Fordham Road leadoff man was already in the batter's box, bat held high. Michael went into his windup and threw strike one. Now the cheer from inside Yankee Stadium was for him.